THE GAUNT WOMAN

JOHN BLACKBURN was born in 1923 in the village of Corbridge, England, the second son of a clergyman. Blackburn attended Haileybury College near London beginning in 1937, but his education was interrupted by the onset of World War II; the shadow of the war, and that of Nazi Germany, would later play a role in many of his works. He served as a radio officer during the war in the Mercantile Marine from 1942 to 1945, and resumed his education afterwards at Durham University, earning his bachelor's degree in 1949. Blackburn taught for several years after that, first in London and then in Berlin, and married Joan Mary Clift in 1950. Returning to London in 1952, he took over the management of Red Lion Books.

It was there that Blackburn began writing, and the immediate success in 1958 of his first novel, *A Scent of New-Mown Hay*, led him to take up a career as a writer full time. He and his wife also maintained an antiquarian bookstore, a secondary career that would inform some of Blackburn's work, including the bibliomystery *Blue Octavo* (1963). *A Scent of New-Mown Hay* typified the approach that would come to characterize Blackburn's twenty-eight novels, which defied easy categorization in their unique and compelling mixture of the genres of science fiction, horror, mystery, and thriller. Many of Blackburn's best novels came in the late 1960s and early 1970s, with a string of successes that included the classics *A Ring of Roses* (1965), *Children of the Night* (1966), *Nothing but the Night* (1968; adapted for a 1973 film starring Christopher Lee and Peter Cushing), *Devil Daddy* (1972) and *Our Lady of Pain* (1974). Somewhat unusually for a popular horror writer, Blackburn's novels were not only successful with the reading public but also won widespread critical acclaim: the *Times Literary Supplement* declared him 'today's master of horror' and compared him with the Grimm Brothers, while the *Penguin Encyclopedia of Horror and the Supernatural* regarded him as 'certainly the best British novelist in his field' and the *St James Guide to Crime & Mystery Writers* called him 'one of England's best practicing novelists in the tradition of the thriller novel'.

By the time Blackburn published his final novel in 1985, much of his work was already out of print, an inexplicable neglect that continued until Valancourt began republishing his novels in 2013. John Blackburn died in 1993.

By John Blackburn

A Scent of New-Mown Hay (1958)*
A Sour Apple Tree (1958)*
Broken Boy (1959)*
Dead Man Running (1960)*
The Gaunt Woman (1962)*
Blue Octavo (1963)*
Colonel Bogus (1964)*
The Winds of Midnight (1964)*
A Ring of Roses (1965)*
Children of the Night (1966)*
The Flame and the Wind (1967)*
Nothing but the Night (1968)*
The Young Man from Lima (1968)
Bury Him Darkly (1969)*
Blow the House Down (1970)*
The Household Traitors (1971)*
Devil Daddy (1972)*
For Fear of Little Men (1972)*
Deep Among the Dead Men (1973)
Our Lady of Pain (1974)*
Mister Brown's Bodies (1975)
The Face of the Lion (1976)*
The Cyclops Goblet (1977)*
Dead Man's Handle (1978)
The Sins of the Father (1979)
A Beastly Business (1982)*
A Book of the Dead (1984)*
The Bad Penny (1985)*

* Available from Valancourt Books

JOHN BLACKBURN

The Gaunt Woman

VALANCOURT BOOKS

The Gaunt Woman by John Blackburn
Originally published in Great Britain by Jonathan Cape in 1962
First U.S. edition published by Mill & Morrow in 1962
First Valancourt Books edition 2024

Published by Valancourt Books, Richmond, Virginia
http://www.valancourtbooks.com

ISBN 978-1-960241-35-1 (*trade paperback*)
Also available as an electronic book.

Cover by Pedro Marques
Set in Dante MT

CHAPTER I

At nine o'clock sharp Sir Martin Rolfe, Chief Financial Adviser to Her Majesty's Treasury, was at his desk. By eleven he had read and answered the thirty-two letters which required his personal attention, and spoken to the Minister, to an Air Chief Marshal, and to a trade union leader on the telephone. By twelve he had given his comments on a road development scheme, two defence estimates, and a pay claim in nationalized industries; total sum involved—a hundred and thirty million pounds. At exactly one minute past twelve he initialled the last folder and closed it.

"Well, that seems to be the lot." Rolfe's voice had every trick of modulation that Winchester, Cambridge, and generations of security could give, but it sounded like a machine, a beautifully tuned instrument which could repeat sounds but had no life of its own. "Yes, that should be quite satisfactory, I think."

He pushed the file away from him and leaned back in his chair, feeling the tiny stab of pain that the least effort seemed to cause him nowadays: too many conferences, too many decisions to be made, too many memories; too much of one memory in particular. He put the last thought quickly from his mind and reached towards the box his secretary held out to him.

"Thank you, Mr. Arabin." He took a cigarette and lit it with his own lighter. This was the end of the ritual which told him his morning's work was finished. He waited impatiently for the man to gather up the papers and leave him to his own thoughts for half an hour—almost the only waking period he allowed to them.

"Excuse me, sir. I hate to bother you with something which is probably trivial, but—" Michael Arabin spoke slowly and carefully as always. He had been over two years in England, but he still had to be careful. Figures were easy to him, of course—figures and balance sheets added up the same way in any language, and he could read them like a novel. But the turn of a phrase, the exact meaning and pronunciation of a word still so often evaded him, and he spoke slowly and carefully, as if his job depended on it—as it probably did. His employer was not a man to suffer fools gladly.

"Well, what is it, Mr. Arabin?" Rolfe pulled hard at his cigarette, watching the grey smoke drifting upwards to the ceiling like the trail of the lost years which had made him what he was. Yes, always upwards: honorary professor of a Cambridge college, chairman of twenty committees, author of a dozen standard works on economics, chief financial adviser to the British Treasury.

"I thought that was the last of them."

"Yes, sir, the last of the official correspondence, that is." Arabin reached in his pocket and placed something on the desk.

"This came in the morning post, sir. As I said, it is probably of no importance, but I didn't like to open it."

"No, I can see that for myself." Rolfe leaned forward, looking at the envelope in front of him. It was crumpled and stained and looked quite out of place against the gleaming mahogany of the desk, the snow-white blotter, and the shining row of pens. The address was written in a sprawling hand that might have belonged to a child or to a very old and feeble person. *Sir Martin Rolfe—c/o the Home Office*. Above the address there was another line printed in thick black ink: LET HIM OPEN THIS HIMSELF IF YOU VALUE YOUR JOBS.

"How very curious, Mr. Arabin." The man had been with him for some time now, but Rolfe would never think of dropping the formal title.

"The warning seems a little stronger than normal, but it will be one of the usual things, I suppose, the work of a lunatic or a beggar. How many did we get last month? Seventeen, I seem to remember. What poor, foolish people there are in the world." He picked it up and reached for his paper knife.

"Yes, sir, you're most probably right. All the same—" Arabin broke off slightly and there was an odd look of embarrassment on his face. "All the same," he repeated, "I wouldn't open it if I were you. I'd just put it in the fire. You see, when I was a young man I studied calligraphy, and there's something about that writing I don't like. I think it shows a lot of hatred." He watched Rolfe's hand sliding the knife into the flap of the envelope, and he thought of the coldness of the man, and the ruthlessness of him, and the long years he had spent climbing up to his present position. He must have made a lot of enemies on his way, a whole army with reasons for hating Sir Martin Rolfe.

"Do you really think so, Mr. Arabin? How very interesting." Rolfe smiled slightly and started to cut the flap with a slow, deliberate movement. "Your concern for my welfare does you credit, but what do you really imagine we are going to find? A poisoned needle to prick my thumb, perhaps? A sheet of blotting paper soaked in germ culture? . . . No, you are a Hungarian, Mr. Arabin, and though these things may happen in your country for all I know, we are in England now." He pulled a single page of crumpled greyish paper from the envelope and started to read. Like the address, the writing was in that strangely childish or senile hand. He was still smiling as he read.

And all at once, quite suddenly and without any warning, something began to happen to Rolfe's face. The smile left those carved, academic features and they went slack. The eyes seemed to glaze over, the thin mouth fell open, and a long gasp came from deep down in his body. For perhaps five seconds he sat like that, quite still and staring at the letter, and then, as though it were the hardest and most important action of his life, he reached for the cigarette lighter. The sheet of paper curled, darkened, and glowed orange. As he watched it, he suddenly seemed to see a face in that flame. The face was his own and it was melting.

"God!" he said, quite oblivious of Arabin standing beside him. "God! God! Dear God!" Over and over again he said it. Then the room dimmed and swung sideways, something that felt like a steel spike started to come out through the centre of his chest, and he fell to the floor.

Freude schöner Götterfunken
Tochter aus Elysium—

Nicholas Malendin, sometime gunner's mate on the Imperial Russian battleship *Tsarevitch,* did not believe in God, but he was very fond of classical music.

He half sat, half lay back in his big chair by the window, staring out over the Kremlin skyline, and there was a look of pure pleasure in his eyes though he couldn't smile. By and large the plastic surgeons had done a wonderful job on his face but there was still a certain stiffness about it when the wind was cold. From the other side of the vast room of plush and gilt a record player gave a surprisingly noisy rendering of Beethoven's *Ninth Symphony,* and Malendin's right leg beat in time to the music. His left was stretched stiffly in front of him, for it was steel and its original had been buried years ago under the rubble of Stalingrad. The highest decoration of the state gleamed on his chest and his shoulders bore the epaulets of a colonel, but these weren't the important things about Malendin. The important thing was a little plastic card in his pocket which named him head of Department 5 of M.V.D., that section of the Soviet Intelligence Service dealing with Western Europe.

Alle Menschen werden Brüder
Wo dein sanfter Flügel weilt.

The chorus climbed to its final climax and the record ground into silence. With surprising agility for his seventy-four years and crippled body, Malendin pulled himself out of his chair and crossed to a telephone by the desk. The phone was fitted with a light instead of a bell, for he hated unnecessary noise, and the light had been flashing for the last three minutes. He was quite aware of this but would never have dreamed of interrupting Beethoven. Besides, until ten seconds ago the time had been part of his lunch break and like a good Socialist he stuck to the terms of his agreement.

"Oh, it's you, Peter," he said, lifting the receiver. "Yes, I want to see you for a few minutes. Something rather interesting has come up." The scar tissue beneath his eyes forced itself into a crinkle, for his caller was an old friend and he had dropped the formal address of "Comrade" years ago.

"Yes, come up right away, please. I'll look forward to seeing you—have a drink waiting as well." He replaced the phone and dragged his steel foot to a cabinet in the corner of the room. He hummed slightly as he did so, and as he lifted out bottle and glasses he looked exactly what he was not: a jovial old gentleman without a care in the world or an unpleasant thought in his head.

The man who came into the room a moment later was of medium build, medium-coloured, and just approaching middle age. His hair was starting to thin and he wore a dark, rather shabby suit with leather-bound elbows. He had a wife and two children whom he adored, and he lived in a flat which he was constantly redecorating. His job fascinated him, but he would never get to the top, for he was without ambition. Men like him could be seen in any suburban train anywhere in the world; he was the typical high-ranking subordinate, the first assistant, the right-hand man who stuck to the book and the rules of the job—any job. His name was Peter Vanin and in his time he had killed two women and more men than he cared to remember—one of them with his bare hands.

"Ah, there you are, Peter. Come in and sit down. Family all right? Good." Malendin pushed a glass towards him and raised his own. "Well, here's luck to both of us."

Malendin threw back the vodka in a single, practised movement and eased himself comfortably in the chair. There was a big buff folder on the desk and he picked it up, balancing it in his hand for a moment.

"This came in yesterday," he said, "from the Hungarians, as it happens, which is in itself an extraordinary thing. Our loyal allies are usually so reluctant to part with any crumbs they manage to pick up. It may be of no value at all, or it could be very useful: a lever to cause a great deal of trouble in certain quarters. I'll give you the details in a moment, but first I want an opinion from you. You are said to have the knack of summing up a person's character from his face, so tell me about this man. What do you see in this face?"

"Very well, I'll have a try, Colonel, but I'm not a miracle worker." Vanin took the photograph Malendin handed him from the file and held it to the light. It was a very studied photograph showing a tall man in a beautifully cut suit standing before a table with a pile of books beside him. The photographer had gone to a lot of trouble to get just the right amount of strength and honesty and friendliness into that wide, posed smile.

"Yes, a very bright boy." Vanin's hand drummed quietly on the desk as he studied the picture.

"He is either British or American and nearer sixty than fifty," Vanin went on. "He is running to fat, but until a few years ago was probably very thin. He is used to power, but I should say that his power comes through people rather than over them. He is probably the possessor of some highly specialized skill. There is also something I don't trust in the face; no, not exactly dishonesty, but I wouldn't rely on him. I would say that he is hiding something all the time."

"Good, Peter." Malendin's voice had the hearty ring of the schoolmaster complimenting a prize pupil. "Now, tell me something else. Could this man be broken?"

"Could he be broken?" Vanin raised his eyebrows slightly. "Yes, of course. As you know, anybody can be broken—if one finds the right pressures, that is. All the same—" he shook his head as he studied the photograph—"I don't think this man would break easily. Who is he, Colonel, and why does he interest us?"

"His name is Sir Martin Rolfe and you should have heard of him." Malendin pulled a sheet of typescript from his folder. "He is an economist and, if we play our cards right, he may become a very valuable ally."

"May he indeed! Yes, I seem to remember the name." Vanin took the paper and, as he read, the photograph seemed to become a living person. "As I said, a bright boy. Fellow of Blenheim College, Cambridge, 1925 to '30—Visiting Professor at Detroit University to '38—Civil Servant in the Ministry of Supply during the war—Permanent Secretary for five years after that. A full life: publications include 'An Approach to Economic Regeneration,' 'The Avoidance or Cure of Diminishing Returns.' Present positions held—Emeritus Professor of Blenheim College and Financial Adviser to the British Treasury. . . . Yes, an important man, Colonel, but why the sudden interest in him now? I'm also curious to know why you used the term 'ally.' A man like that could only be our bitterest enemy."

"Quite right on the surface, Peter, but only on the surface. People change, you know, and their views and loyalties alter. Well, I wonder if it might be possible to change the loyalties of Sir Martin Rolfe."

"Go on, Colonel, you're beginning to interest me."

"Thank you, I was hoping I might." Malendin's hand ran slowly across his cheek. The skin beneath it felt strangely like tissue paper.

"Now," he went on, "we know that Rolfe is a very able and influential man. As an economist he is trusted by the British Government and holds the position of Chief Financial Adviser to the Treasury. More important than that, the Minister, Lord Tremayne, is said to rely on him completely. And, at the end of this month, Tremayne goes to Washington for a conference concerning the pound-dollar exchange rate. Rolfe goes with him: the British line will be exactly what Rolfe suggests."

"And so?"

"And so, my dear Peter, I've been wondering. I've been wondering if it might not be possible to sabotage that conference. Tremayne is a politician, not an economist, and he will take whatever advice Rolfe gives him. Well, suppose Rolfe gave the wrong advice—suppose they tried to push the Americans too far, and set the pound at an absurdly high figure. Then I think we might be hitting them where it really hurts—at home and in their pockets. Yes, we might hurt the British Lion very badly without anyone knowing we had a hand in it. As their own saying goes, 'There are more ways of killing a cat than choking it with cream.' I can see some interesting possibilities, Peter."

"So can I." Vanin considered for a moment, and he saw quite clearly what Malendin meant: the pound and the British bank rate set far too high, the flow of foreign money into Britain cut off as though by a tap. He saw Britain's production slowing down because its goods were too expensive to sell, and the British unemployment figures starting to grow. The consequences were clear—closed factories, and strikes, and industrial unrest. And, at the end, a general election with a left-wing, pacifist government coming home at a canter. The dream of the Department for years: no more rocket bases on British soil and the end of the Anglo-American alliance once and for all.

"But why, Colonel?" Vanin asked. "Why should Rolfe give the wrong advice?"

"Perhaps because I ask him to give it." Malendin smiled and suddenly he looked like a cat who knows the mouse is very near.

"A little bird told me something about Rolfe, Peter. He told me that the man is frightened of something—he is terrified out of his wits. And if we could learn what frightens him, if we knew that, then I wouldn't be a bit surprised if Sir Martin Rolfe didn't do exactly what I told him to do." The smile left his face and when he spoke again he was simply the professional policeman marshalling his facts.

"There is a man in London called Arabin," he said. "Michael Arabin, a Hungarian traitor who got out of the country during the last uprising. He thought that his family had got out too, by another route, but he was wrong. They are still in Budapest and this makes Arabin a very unhappy man. To cut the story short, Arabin settled in England and got a job as Rolfe's secretary. He is an economist himself, and Rolfe is the kind of man who would employ a refugee rather than a fellow countryman. At any rate, Arabin has worked for Rolfe for over nine months.

"Now, those are all the facts we have been able to check on. For the rest we merely have Arabin's word. It seems that a week ago he called at the Hungarian Embassy in London and spoke to their security officer. He told him that he had an important piece of information regarding Rolfe which he was prepared to sell. The price was his family being allowed to leave Hungary."

"I see." For a second Vanin considered his own family. He imagined that in similar circumstances he might act very much as Arabin had done. "What was Arabin's information, Colonel?"

"He told the Hungarians that during the last six weeks Rolfe has been receiving certain letters which might well be the build-up to a blackmail attempt. At any rate the man is terrified of them. The first one was enough to give him a minor heart attack. Arabin's description of his opening it was rather vivid. He said Rolfe looked like a devil that had been too long in the fire. When he had read it, he just managed to burn it and then he fainted."

"Did he indeed?" Vanin glanced at the photograph before him. "I'd be very interested to know what that letter contained. As I said, I don't think this man would break easily."

"But according to Arabin he is breaking up now. Since the first letter arrived there have been three more, and Rolfe is going to pieces; hardly eats at all, sleeps badly, relies on drugs to keep him going. . . .

"No, there doesn't seem to have been any demand for money as yet," Malendin continued. "Arabin says he is almost sure that Rolfe doesn't even know the identity of the writer. Arabin can't swear to it, of course, but he thinks that only the last letter could have contained an address."

"The last letter! You mean—" Vanin leaned forward in his chair.

"Yes, we have that letter all right. Arabin got his hands on it eight days ago, but he didn't give it to Rolfe. He stole it from Rolfe's desk and handed it over to the Hungarians as proof of his good faith, though he removed the address. He will let us have the address in return for his family." Malendin pulled half a sheet of greyish paper from his folder. He looked slightly embarrassed as he handed it to Vanin.

"This seems crazy, Peter, but we have to be sure. Very possibly it's just a hoax on Arabin's part, but we must know."

"Yes, we have to know everything in our job, don't we?" Vanin grinned and took the paper. It was stained and crumpled and had been cut across the top. There were just two lines of sprawling writing and a matchstick drawing that might have been done by a child. The drawing showed a tall figure in a skirt standing before a shop window. There was a rope tied in a noose round the figure's neck and the words above the drawing read *I am still thinking of the Gaunt Woman who can blast you.*

"The Gaunt Woman—well, well! And this piece of nonsense, or something like it, was enough to give Martin Rolfe, the great economist, a heart attack." Once again Vanin glanced at the photograph. "I wonder what you've been up to, my friend. I really wonder. . . .

"Well, Colonel, just where are we?" Vanin said. "This is either a hoax on Arabin's part, or somebody with a rather nasty sense of humour has got his hooks into Rolfe. I don't think it's a hoax, either. If Arabin had wanted to invent something, he'd have been much more subtle. Have our handwriting people seen this yet?"

"Oh, yes, and I've been through their report. The note appears to have been written by an old person in poor health. The writer was probably male, though they're not certain about that. They seem sure of the type of person though. Whoever wrote this, Peter, was mentally ill. . . .

"It's intriguing, isn't it? A lunatic did this. A very powerful lunatic, though, with something very important to tell us. And, if we could find that lunatic, Peter—if we could find him and make him tell us what that something is . . . then I might hold Sir Martin Rolfe in the hollow of my hand." Malendin laid his hand on the desk as he spoke and slowly flexed his fingers: a hard, strong hand that would finish a job whatever the circumstances. "I'll get through to Budapest at once, I think. Tell them we'll take over this business and they can let Arabin know he'll be having a visitor. . . .

"No, I don't think I want to involve any of our regular groups in England. Our colleagues of the British Intelligence Service are good, and we can't afford the risk. It'll have to be someone sent out from here, I'm afraid. Someone who knows England well, but hasn't been there for a long time. Someone who speaks English well enough to at least pass as an American. Someone I can rely on completely. You understand, don't you, Peter?"

"Yes, I understand you." Vanin watched his face and all at once the slightly cynical expression left Malendin's eyes and he looked what he really was—a machine, or part of a machine. A cog that had been designed in the days of violence and went on turning as its makers intended—which would go on turning like that till it wore out or was destroyed. Policies might alter, politicians might change, but the department didn't alter and men like Malendin didn't change. His face was that of one of the old, unrelenting Bolsheviks—the fanatic who couldn't stop, for he had sounded on the trumpet that would never call retreat.

"Yes, there's only one choice, isn't there, Colonel?" Vanin smiled slightly as he spoke with the prompt, accepting smile of the permanent official, the professional who did exactly what the job told him to do.

"I'm right, Peter, though personally I'm very sorry. In a way this is police work and you were a detective once. You were in London on our embassy staff during the war. Also you are a married man."

"Yes, I'm a married man." Though they were old friends, Vanin understood the threat perfectly. Any failure or desertion on his part would be rewarded in the usual way. "When do you want me to leave?"

"Let's see." Malendin opened his drawer and consulted a battered notebook.

"Rolfe leaves for Washington on the twenty-eighth, which gives us very little time. All the same, I don't want you to take any chances. The western route will be best, I think. Yes, there is a reconnaissance trawler leaving Archangelsk next Friday. That will do nicely. We'll have two days to work out contacts and papers. I'll see that our people over there give you full co-operation, but don't use them more than you need. As I said, the British Intelligence is good—very good." He stood up and held out his hand; then he watched Vanin move to the door. Just before he reached it, Malendin called him back.

"Peter," he said, "you may be going on a wild goose chase, or you may not be. And if you're not, I want that information, I want it very badly indeed. I also want you to remember one thing. People lock valuables up in safes. Well, safes may be little tin boxes or great steel and concrete vaults, but they always have one thing in common: a door and a key to open it.

"And that's what I want from you, Peter. I want a key. I want the knowledge of that old and mentally sick person which is the key to Sir Martin Rolfe. I don't mind how you get it, but find me that key. . . . Goodbye for the present."

He watched the door close behind the man he might well be sending to his death, and then he went back to the desk and poured himself another drink. As he did so his eyes fell on the sheet of paper and the little matchstick drawing. He smiled and raised his glass to the photograph beside it.

"Well, Sir Martin," he said. "Here's to her! Here's to the Gaunt Woman who can blast you!"

CHAPTER II

Fog like smoke above the hills, a gun firing every ninety seconds from the cliffs, and, out to sea, a dark shape rising and falling on the Atlantic swell. Western Ireland and the Soviet trawler *Luba K* coming in against the tide.

The naval lieutenant leaned against the wheelhouse bulkhead and was almost blind in the night and the fog, but that didn't worry him in the slightest. He trusted his navigation. He trusted his radar. Besides, the signal gun from the light house on shore told him exactly where he was. The thing that worried him was the normal headache of every Russian sea captain off a foreign coast—the constant threat of desertion. The ship was still two miles out, but already most of the crew were confined to quarters.

Once again the gun boomed out across the water, and his hand came hard down on the engine telegraph. Then he turned to the man at his side.

"All right, Comrade, this is it. A couple of miles over there is Mizzen Head, where we part company." There was no trace of regret in his voice, for like all sailors he was superstitious. He had carried these people before, and he thought of them as Jonahs, bringers of bad luck. At the moment he had just one wish: to put a few more sea miles between the shore and the ambitions of his crew. "You all ready?"

"Yes, I'm ready." Peter Vanin looked at the suitcase at his feet. It, and the clothes he wore, had been bought six months ago in a New York store for just such an emergency. Together with the papers in his pocket, they proclaimed him an American tourist recently landed at Shannon. He also had a wallet containing a book of traveller's checks. And beside the wallet there rested a big, old-fashioned fountain pen. That pen had taken several months of a craftsman's life to perfect and, if one knew its secret, it could do rather more than write. A slight twist on the body and the nib mechanism would slide back to show the open muzzle behind it. It fired three soft-nosed bullets and was a very horrible little weapon in the hands of a professional. These were all that Vanin had: his tools against the West.

There was also one other piece of equipment that couldn't be described as a tool, though it was just as basic—a little plastic cylinder screwed to Vanin's back teeth. Colonel Malendin was a careful man, and his agents took no chances. If things went wrong, one bite on that cylinder would put a stop to all questions and all fear.

"Yes, I'm ready, Comrade Lieutenant," he said again, knowing that it was a lie, that he wasn't ready; that his body was tired, and he'd sat too long in offices for this sort of job. All the same, it was his job, and his body would just have to make the best of it.

"Let's go, shall we?" Vanin picked up the case and moved out of the wheelhouse, feeling the fog like a blanket across his face and hearing the gun bellow again across the water, then its long echo from the hills behind. The signal station must be almost dead ahead and he supposed they would go on firing till the fog lifted. With its engines cut, the trawler seemed like a little burnt-out world, a space ship doomed to drift forever in a vacuum. It was a cramped, uncomfortable world, but at least warm, and he hated to leave it.

"You'll put a good man in the boat, won't you?" Vanin asked.

"Yes, don't worry about that." The lieutenant looked at the shadowy figures lowering the dinghy into the water, his mind on his own worry. The constant dread that, one day, enough would-be deserters might lead to mutiny.

"My bosun, Matushenko, is taking you over. He's been with

this old tub since she was first commissioned and you can rely on him all right. His main problem will be to find his way back to us when he's put you ashore." He took Vanin's case and dropped it down to a man in the boat. Then he held out his hand.

"Still, that's not your problem, Comrade," he said, feeling the slight tremble in Vanin's fingers and the coldness of his grip. Though the lieutenant's one ambition was to get rid of his charge quickly, there was a sudden pity in his eyes.

"Well, goodbye now, and good luck. Lots of luck, though I hope you won't need it." He watched Vanin swing out onto the rope ladder; then he moved back into the chart room to make out his log. One stuck to the rules in the Soviet service and every event had to be punctually recorded.

The fog seemed much thinner in the boat, swirling above them in streams but leaving a clear gap over the water, and Vanin could see the full length of the dinghy quite clearly. He settled himself back in the bow and watched his companion cast off and start the well-silenced motor. An old, old sailor, this Matushenko, almost ready for retirement, and like himself a professional. He would find the beach all right; there was nothing to worry about on that score. The only worry was—who would be there to meet him. Vanin had no illusions about the efficiency of the Western intelligence services, and already there might be a little group of shadowy figures standing in the fog waiting for him. To steady his nerves, he lit a cigarette and pulled hard at it against the drag of the damp air, listening to the whine of the motor and the sough of the bow cutting across the long swell.

No, there was no need to worry yet. Everything had been planned to the last detail. An agent would meet him at the top of the cliffs and they would go to London together: it was safer that way. And, in London, if things went wrong, he could get any help he needed from the office. Gregor Tanek would see to that. He knew Tanek well: a fat, jolly, dissolute man with a taste for blonde women as large as himself and for English lyric poetry. A good man, though, one of the best they had in Western Europe. He could rely on full support from Gregor Tanek.

The real work, however, was all his own. He had to find Rolfe's letter writer and get the necessary information from him. Then he had to break Rolfe in good time for the conference and hand him over to a financial expert from the embassy. A lot to do and only five days to do it in.

He lowered his head below the spirals of mist and leaned back in his seat, thinking of his plans and hearing the gun fire again from the cliffs. As the last echo died he suddenly looked up with a jerk and knew that something was wrong.

"All right, Comrade," his companion was saying, "this is it. This is where you get out and walk." Matushenko's hand cut the engine and the boat drifted into the trough of a wave. His words were slow and careful as though they had been rehearsed for a long time. They had only been travelling a few minutes and there was still a good mile to the shore.

"What's the matter? Have you gone crazy?" Vanin started to say, and then he saw the revolver in the man's hand. An old revolver, like Matushenko himself—heavy and outdated, but still lethal. It must have been treasured and hidden away for just such an emergency.

"You'll never get away with it, you fool—never in a thousand years!"

"Yes, I'll get away with it all right, Comrade." The man's voice was strangely indifferent, as though he were merely stating facts which could not be denied. "There's nothing to stop me except you, is there? Once ashore, I'll go to that lighthouse and give myself up. They'll look after me all right. They always look after our people who go over to them."

"But why, Matushenko? Why should a man like you want to desert? A man with your record—with your name?" As he spoke, Vanin arched his body for a spring, but at the same moment he knew it was useless. He would be dead before he left his seat.

"Yes, I've got a good record, haven't I, Comrade? And mine's a famous name too. Matushenko; I should be proud of it. The same name as that Afanasy Matushenko who led the mutineers on the *Potemkin* in 1905. The man who was hanged by his own countrymen. All the same, I have reasons for what I'm doing, Comrade—I have good reasons."

"But what about your family? They're still in Russia, aren't they? You know what will happen to them if you desert." Vanin was thinking of his own family as he spoke.

"No. I haven't got a family, Comrade." Matushenko shook his head slightly. "Both my sons were killed in the war, and my wife died last voyage. The doctor told me she was going to die, but they wouldn't let me stay with her. I begged the port captain to let me stay, but he wouldn't listen. He just handed me over to a political commissar who gave me a nice, friendly lecture on my duty to the Party and Mother Russia. My wife died alone, Comrade."

The big gun started to come up as he spoke. "No, I've nothing to lose, and nobody will suffer from what I do. Now, how do you want it, Comrade, in the front or in the back?"

"In the front, Matushenko, but listen to me first. Give me just one minute." Vanin struggled to put just the right plea into his voice. It wasn't difficult. He meant every word he said.

"I *have* got a family, you see—a wife and two kids. Let me write to them, please—just a few lines. I'll give you the address and you could post it when you've got ashore. It won't cost you anything—only the price of a stamp. Please let me do that."

"All right, Comrade, you can write your letter. Just a few lines though, and don't try anything. If you make one wrong move I'll shoot you in the guts and you know what that feels like, don't you?" As he spoke the signal gun fired again, and the revolver moved up and down like a pointer in his hand.

"No, I won't try anything." Vanin pulled out a packet of cigarettes and took out their contents. "You might as well have these," he said, laying them on the seat and tearing open the empty packet to provide a writing surface. Then he reached in his pocket for the big fountain pen. It felt like lead as he twisted the cap and made the nib swing sideways.

"I won't be a moment." Vanin leaned forward slightly, as though considering what to write, till the pen was pointing just where he wanted it. The business was almost finished. He had only to press the switch and Matushenko would be done for.

But quite suddenly, as he looked at that heavy, stupid, and rather kindly face, Vanin felt that he couldn't kill the man. He had sat too long in an office and grown too soft to kill anybody again. He was facing a deserter who pointed a gun at his heart, but he couldn't kill him, for he was a desk man without strength or courage. Whatever the book or the rules of the department said, he wouldn't shoot to kill. Vanin began to lower his hand till it was aimed at the man's wrist.

But—*the rules and the book!* Like a voice in his ear, like a sudden flash of inspiration, he saw how it was and the weapon came up again. He didn't want to kill, but then he, Peter Vanin, didn't have to. Peter Vanin didn't exist as a person at all. He was just a part of the machine, a cog in the organization, and he didn't matter. Only the rules and the book mattered; it was they who were going to kill Matushenko, for they had sentenced him to death. He braced his arm, waited for the next report of the signal gun, and pressed the switch. With no fuss and hardly any noise the thing he held exploded, and it was finished. Matushenko still sat where he was, but the revolver was lying at his feet and he looked quite different. He had three eyes now; one was almost in the centre of his forehead. He did not appear to bleed a great deal.

And that was that. There was no need for reproach, though Vanin felt slightly sick as he looked at that slumped body, so altered in death. He had done exactly what the book said he should do, and now he had to get on with the real work. He moved forward and pulled Matushenko to one side. Then he started the engine. There was a compass beside the tiller and he steered for the east.

The beach was exactly what he had hoped for: soft sand that held the boat firmly, and here and there scattered rocks that looked like small, grazing animals in the thinning mist. He took a knife from Matushenko's belt and very carefully cut holes in the buoyancy tanks; then he lashed the body to its seat. When it was quite secure he piled a heap of stones on the duckboards and removed the draining plug.

Everything was in order again and he had done just what the book said he should do. He was a little late for his appointment, and Lieutenant Golinoff had lost a good sailor, but that was all. He started the motor, threw it into reverse, and watched the boat begin to move out to sea. She would sink in deep water and nobody would tell any tales. He picked up his case and began to walk up the beach.

He had made a good landfall, it seemed, and he found the path without difficulty. It was just a sheep track winding up through a gap in the cliffs, the tufts of grass underfoot here and there covered by scree falls that felt like knives beneath his thin city shoes. Already there was a faint glow in the East, and the fog was breaking up fast. Beyond the piled rocks he could make out the loom of mountains, and all around was the smell of sheep and pinewoods and the sound of running water. When the signal gun fired again, it sounded almost on top of him. The lighthouse must be just round the next break in the cliffs. With his feet slipping and stumbling on the slope he struggled upwards—and then paused for a moment as his case collided with something at the side of the track and was dragged from his hand. He bent down and looked at the thing that had caused it: a little stone pillar with lettering half hidden by the salt and lichens that covered it. BRIAN CONNOR—BORN 1900, MURDERED 1922—HE DIED FOR IRELAND.

Died for Ireland! In Vanin's present state of mind, with nothing but those dripping cliffs around him and the hint of low, somehow ignoble mountains ahead, Ireland seemed rather an unworthy cause to die for. He shook his head slightly and hurried on upwards to the place where his contact had been told to meet him. A few yards further on, the path made a final turn to the right and the cliffs ran out into flat moorland. As he negotiated this stretch, Vanin suddenly stopped dead, staring up at the things before him. There was a little ticking pulse in his forehead which came from fear as well as from exhaustion.

The three men hung from their crosses, and for a moment they seemed to be alive—horribly alive. Vanin put down his case, for he knew where he was. This was the rendezvous that had been described to him, and he knew that such calvaries were common in Ireland. All the same, the sight still shocked him. There was something too lifelike in those marble figures straining from their nails, with tortured faces turned out towards the Atlantic. He stood quite still for a moment, looking up at the Calvary, feeling more alone than he had ever felt in his life, but knowing that he wasn't alone. The only movements around him were the slight whisper of wind and, here and there, the shapes of grazing sheep—but he wasn't alone. Somewhere human eyes were watching him, as they had been trained and told to watch. He couldn't pray, but he hoped they were the right eyes.

For perhaps ten seconds he stood like that, recalling his instruction and the prepared words. Then he walked forward to the most westerly cross and looked up at the face of the dying thief. Rather horribly, it reminded him of Matushenko.

"Lord," he said to the damp air, and the carved stone, and the thin, winter sun coming up over the hills. It was the first time he had ever spoken the word aloud.

"Lord, remember me when thou comest into thy kingdom." He heard a slight movement as he spoke.

"Yes, quite correct, and almost on time too." The voice was just behind the centre cross. *"Today thou shalt be with me in paradise."*

The woman stepped out from a pile of rocks behind the Calvary and she was tall and dark, with her hair tied back under a scarf. She wore slacks and a belted raincoat and in the drifting mist she could have been a creature from a fairy tale.

Her face might have been beautiful if there had been a little less strength in it.

"Good morning to you," she said, and held out her hand. Her grip was pleasant and warm, and full of confidence. Vanin felt better for it.

"My name is Kate Reilly. I hope you had a pleasant journey." She smiled as she spoke and, though he saw the faint mockery in that smile, he didn't mind it. He thought of the roped body drifting out to sea, and he was suddenly glad that Tanek had sent a woman to meet him.

"Mine is Peter Vanin."

"Yes, I know, and I've been very thoroughly briefed about you. You are my second cousin from New York City and your occupation is journalism. You are over here on a holiday, but you are also looking for copy. I am to take you to London and act as your assistant and general contact. That's all they told me. Would you like to give me a few more details before we start?"

"No, not at the moment." He gave a tolerant shrug of his shoulders against all female curiosity. "As it happens, I have very few details myself."

"I see. Then let's go, shall we? I've got a car parked about a mile away, and we have to catch the afternoon plane from Dublin." She watched him reach for his case and then smiled again.

"Tell me, Mr. Vanin—or perhaps I'd better start calling you Peter—does it worry you that I'm a woman?"

"No, it doesn't worry me. It doesn't worry me at all. As long as you're efficient." As he looked at her, he knew that the remark was quite unnecessary. Even if she tried, this woman could never be anything else except efficient. "All the same, if we're to work together, I'd like to know a little more about you. You're not one of us, but English or Irish. Just why were you picked for the job?"

"Perhaps because I *am* Irish." She turned away from him and looked out towards the sea as she spoke. "I am also a landscape painter, specializing in this coast. Quite a good one as it happens, and I have a cottage in the next village. That gives me an excellent reason for travelling between here and London. Does that satisfy you?"

"No, not really. I want to know *why*, Kate." Somehow the name came quite naturally to him. "Just why are you working for us? I wouldn't put you down as a keen party member, or even as a sympathizer."

"And you'd be right, Peter, quite right. I work for you for three reasons. The first is money, and the second you may be able to guess. Because of something I did when I was young and filled with an enthusiasm for political causes. I think you understand, don't you, Comrade?" There was a sudden bitterness in her voice.

"Yes." *Something I did when I was young.* As Vanin listened, he knew exactly how it could have been done—how often it was done. Young people with a spirit of revolt following causes, almost for the fun of the thing. Causes which they would one day outgrow, as most of them did outgrow, but some were not allowed to. Some were thought to be useful and these few were flattered and cultivated and paid. Then, one day, when the enthusiasm started to die, the velvet gloves were taken off and the organization showed itself. Something discreditable, or illegal, or merely frightening would be laid at their heels, and they would belong to the Party body and soul.

"Yes, I know how it is," he said. "And what's the third reason?"

"The third reason I don't suppose you'll understand, being a Russian. It's merely because I'm Irish and because of that feel so very, very fond of the English." Her expression altered slightly as she spoke. The look of a mischievous child discussing an unpopular headmaster.

"I understand. Yes, they are a lovable people." Vanin considered the little stone pillar on the path and the message it carried, BRIAN CONNOR—DIED FOR IRELAND.

A stupid people, he thought. A poor, foolish people, carrying on their outdated hate and following any cause, so long as it was directed against England. All the same, sometimes a useful people, for those who knew how to control them.

"Let's go," he said, and picking up the case, began to walk forward.

The sun was already quite high above the hills now, and in the distance he could make out the winding road which would take them to Dublin. This was the real start of the journey and he was quite satisfied. He had made his landfall, Kate should prove a reliable assistant, and the book would never let him down. Tonight he would be amongst his enemies with almost every man's hand against him, but that didn't matter if he only followed the book. He had only to do that and soon he would be standing before Sir Martin Rolfe with the knowledge to break him.

Vanin was right of course—quite right. He was a professional who had been a long time at his trade, and if he played his cards well nothing could stop him. In a short time he would know the meaning of that scrawled letter and its childish drawing that hid Rolfe's probably very nasty secret. There was only one thing which the book couldn't tell him.

The thing was death, and if he made one mistake, one slip in the card game, it would come to him almost automatically. He walked on across the heather towards a car to Dublin, a plane to London, and the little matchstick picture which somebody with a sick mind had called the Gaunt Woman.

CHAPTER III

They exchanged hardly a dozen words in the car, but in the plane they had to talk for the sake of appearances. After a time they talked like people.

Not like real people, of course; that was impossible, for their lives only met in a world of pretence. All the same Vanin was a good inventor and from time to time Kate laughed with genuine amusement as he recounted the history of their American relatives. Maureen Reilly, housemaid of Boston, who married a Polish refugee named Stanislas Vanin back in the eighties—the St. Patrick's night after the war when Uncle Brian missed his footing and fell from a ferryboat between Manhattan and Hoboken—how Aunt Tessie's saloon was doing in Jersey City—

And as she listened, Kate seemed to get quite a different picture of this man whom she had first thought a humourless fanatic. There was a joy in him, a laughing quality hidden away under a very drab exterior. They were just coming into London Airport when she asked a question and saw the laughter switched off like a lamp.

"Tell me, Peter," she said. "I almost forgot to ask you. Is your wife well? I haven't seen her since I was just a child, and can only just remember her."

"My wife?" The good humour left his face, and it seemed revealed as if by the opening of a theatrical backdrop to show nothing but bleakness and loneliness behind.

"Yes, Shura is well enough," he said, knowing that though the answer was true, he couldn't count on it remaining so. Shura and the kids were the only things he had ever loved in his life, but they were also hostages for his good behaviour. Though he and Malendin were old friends, the rules of the department were quite clear. Let him make one bad mistake, show one sign of disloyalty, and the punishment would be automatic. It was not only he who would be punished.

"And thank you for asking." He suddenly hated Kate Reilly for her curiosity, and he turned away, staring down at the approaching runway. Not till the airport bus turned into the terminal did he speak again.

"Well, Kate, here we are," he said, tightening his coat. "And I'd like to say how very glad I am that we were able to meet up again." The cousinly pretence had to be maintained and her question had obviously been quite innocent. Besides, they were working together. All the same—the memory of his family and that little overdecorated flat was like a physical pain in his head. He watched the last of their fellow passengers file off the bus and then stood up.

"And now to business, my dear. I've got your phone number, and I'll get in touch when and if I need you: probably tomorrow morning. Please see that you're always by the phone till twelve noon." He followed her out of the bus, taking his case from a porter, and stared up at the red glow of the London lights. The last time he had seen the city had been in the blackout, and they came as a slight shock—the denial of a memory.

"Well, goodbye for the present, Kate," he said. "I expect we will be meeting again very soon." As though remembering his role and his good manners, he leaned forward and kissed her lightly on the cheek. It was an extremely dutiful and cousinly kiss and meant nothing at all except a slight mockery. Then he turned and walked away—a very ordinary and somehow pathetic figure dragging his case through the London crowds.

Vanin took a room in a small family hotel off the Cromwell Road and he washed and shaved before going to work, for he was that kind of man. Besides there was no need to hurry. British offices didn't shut before five and the person he wanted would still be on duty. Punctually at a quarter to the hour he went out into the street and looked for a phone booth.

"Viaduct double one, double two." Clear and impersonal, a well-trained voice tinkled at the end of the line, and obediently Vanin pressed the button. As he heard the heavy coins fall he wondered how a people that prided itself on freedom could put up with the torture of British currency. "Could I speak to Mr. Michael Arabin, please?"

"Mr. Ar-ab-in." The voice gave the three-syllabled name its full accentuation. "Do you happen to know the number of his extension, sir?"

"No, I'm afraid I don't know that, but you should be able to trace him all right. He is personal assistant to Sir Martin Rolfe."

"Oh, I see. One moment, please." The line seemed to go dead for a moment and then another voice took over.

"Could I have your name, sir, and then I'll enquire if Mr. Arabin is available?"

"Yes, of course; it's Vanin, Peter Vanin." He concentrated on finding a word which would get him connected, and the name of Arabin's wife seemed the obvious choice. "Would you tell him it is about the Magdalena contract, please," he said, hearing the line die again and a third voice come through.

This time he knew it was the voice he wanted; a voice not British in accent, speaking very slowly and carefully and struggling to hide emotion. Struggling unsuccessfully too. Even through the little plastic cap of the phone, Vanin could feel the hope, and excitement, and fear in that careful voice.

"Arabin here," said the voice. "Yes, I have been expecting your call. I would very much like to discuss the terms of our contract as soon as possible. Would this evening be satisfactory?"

"This evening would do very well indeed." Vanin glanced at his watch. "Would you name the time and place, please? Thank you. In one hour, then." He made a neat entry in his notebook and replaced the phone. So far, so good, he thought. He had made his second contact and everything was going according to schedule. In an hour's time he would be talking to the man who owned the piece of paper with the address they wanted. He was also quite sure that Arabin's story was genuine. The tense, excited voice on the phone told him that. He pulled back the door and stepped out of the booth.

"Good evening." The girl who spoke came hurrying towards him across the pavement, and at first he thought she was a prostitute, though of a very curious kind. Her face was without make-up and she wore sandals, a man's flannel trousers, and a worn leather jerkin. Long black hair flowed round her shoulders in uncombed tassels and there was a big sheet of paper in her hand. For a moment he stood staring at her, considering the curious sexual tastes of the British, then he saw the blue-and-white badge on her lapel and began to understand.

"Would you care to sign this petition, sir? It is a protest to the Government on allowing American rocket bases on British soil." She held the paper up to him. It had very few signatures, but a long line of neatly ruled columns. As he looked at it, Vanin grinned and a terrible temptation to make an entry came into his head. *I am strongly against American bases on British soil: Peter Vanin—Department 5 of M.V.D.—Central Intelligence Bureau of the Union of Soviet Socialist Republics.*

"No, I'm sorry," he said, fighting temptation. "I'm afraid it is impossible."

"But why?" The girl's face flushed with annoyance. "Do you want to see our country occupied by foreign troops? You look an intelligent man, so tell me something." She pushed forward as she spoke. Her leather coat smelled like an old, uncared-for horse. "Just what do you think of us? Do you think we're traitors or something?"

"No, I don't think you are traitors." He drew back, looking at the mud-stained feet, the rumpled trousers, and the lank hair.

"All I think, my dear, is that you could do with a bloody good wash." He touched his hat politely and walked away down the street.

The London Underground was quicker than he'd remembered, and he was early getting to the bar where he had arranged to meet Arabin. It stood on a corner at the east end of Oxford Street, and the doors were just opening as he reached it. He bought a paper from the kiosk beside the entrance, and then followed the procession of black-coated, bowler-hatted figures into the saloon, ordering a small whiskey and carrying it to one of the alcoves that ran along the wall. Arabin would not be there for a few minutes, so he opened his paper and glanced idly at the headlines, smiling slightly as he read: KHRUSHCHEV ON THE CARPET BEFORE U.N.; MISTER K'S NEW BLUNDER.

He pushed it away from him and looked at the other occupants of the room. They seemed to be all clerical workers, all middle class, and all in the uniform dress of black and grey. A few sat alone bent over crossword puzzles, but mostly they stood in groups along the bar, discussing office problems, the weather, or the state of the train services to the suburbs. Vanin lifted his glass and silently toasted them.

A nice, but very foolish people who sat on top of a land mine, he thought. Mr. K's Blunder indeed! Didn't they realize that Nikita Khrushchev couldn't blunder, because he was not a man but merely part of the machine that had been tuned and perfected over years? That on the first mistake on his part, Khrushchev would disappear and another cog would take his place—just as there was another cog to replace Peter Vanin and Nicholas Malendin if they blundered.

No, they couldn't know that, any more than they could foresee the economic ruin which this same Peter Vanin was hoping to bring against them; or foresee that, if he played his cards well and got the necessary information on Martin Rolfe, every one of them might be a little poorer before the end of next year. He sipped his drink, smiling at those well-fed, self-confident, but doomed backs, and he felt slightly sorry for them. Then the door opened, and he saw the man he had come to meet walk into the room.

Michael Arabin wore the same clothes as everybody in the bar, but he looked quite different. He stood in the doorway staring around him, and he might have been any age between thirty and fifty, and any one of ten nationalities. Only his expression was typical. That ageless, nationless face bore an expression of cynicism, of weariness, and at the same time of sentimentality—of fanaticism, and the complete acceptance of evil. It was the face of Central Europe.

"Mr. Arabin?" Vanin started to hold out his hand, and then stopped. Something in the man's eyes told him he wouldn't take it.

"Do sit down, please. What will you have to drink?"

"Oh, anything—anything at all." Arabin looked at the glass on the table and shrugged his shoulders. "What are you having? Whiskey; that will do very well." He watched Vanin move towards the bar, and then he took a case from his pocket and lit a cigarette. Somehow it seemed to be holding his face together as he dragged at it.

"Tell me," he said, as Vanin sat down beside him. "I'm afraid I didn't catch your name on the phone—only my wife's name. Are you from the embassy, or did they send you from Budapest?"

"From neither, as it happens. My name is Peter Vanin, and I have come from Moscow." There was no one within earshot of their cubicle and it was safe to talk freely.

"From Moscow! I see. Then that means that your people are—"

"That means that we are interested in your story, nothing more; though we are prepared to talk business. On the other hand, if what you told the Hungarians turns out to be true—if we can find this person who has been writing to Rolfe—if we get enough information to make Rolfe work for us—then we will see that your family are allowed to leave Hungary. You have my word for that."

"Your word!" There was suddenly a lot of hatred in Arabin's eyes.

"My word, Mr. Arabin. You have no choice except to trust us, I'm afraid. After all, we're not animals."

"No, you are not animals, are you?" There was no mistaking the contempt in his voice. "You are Russians."

"Yes, I'm a Russian, Mr. Arabin." Vanin looked away from the man's set face and he suddenly remembered London as he had known it during the war. A drab, scarred city, but a city of friends. Now it was like a great hostile trap shutting him in. "I am also just a man like you who has to do a job. It may possibly interest you to know that I have a family as well. Now, do you want to get down to business or not? If not, you have only to get up and walk out of here. I can't stop you."

"Very well, I'll do business with you." Arabin reached in his pocket and drew out a scrap of paper.

"Here is the address from that letter I gave to the Hungarian Embassy. It's just a *poste restante* address, I'm afraid, but with your great organization,"—his lip curled slightly as he spoke—"it should not be impossible to trace the sender."

"Thank you." Once again Vanin looked at that oddly senile or childish writing; then he folded the paper neatly and put it away in his wallet. "No," he said, "it shouldn't be too difficult to trace him. Tell me something, though. Do you think that Rolfe himself knows of this address?"

"Rolfe does not know, Mr. Vanin, and the fact you asked such a question proves that you know very little about him. This is the fourth letter to reach the office. Rolfe has never seen it, and the other three did not carry an address. I am quite certain about that because, if they had, this one would never have been posted. They couldn't have been, you see. The sender would be dead."

"You mean—"

"I mean that Rolfe would have killed him—or had him killed. Oh, yes, Mr. Vanin, even in law-abiding England, he would have tried to do that. I know my employer and I saw the effect those letters had on him. If he could get his hands on whoever sent them, he would kill that person with about as much compunction as I would kill a rat.

"Now tell me—tell me just what you know about Martin Rolfe. Then I'll try and give you a rather fuller picture." He leaned back, listening, a quiet smile flickering round his eyes, and when Vanin had finished Arabin lifted his glass and drank for the first time.

"I see; and that's all you know, is it? You know the positions he holds. You know of his works on economics. You know about the commissions he has sat on. A lot of those, aren't there: 'Financial Aid to Undeveloped Countries in the Commonwealth'—'An Enquiry into Racial Discrimination in Britain.' . . . Yes, my employer has sat on a great many commissions, and he is a very influential man. He needs influence, I think. He craves it as some people want drink or drugs or power. It's an obsession with him, this wish to persuade people to follow his lead. Take this conference in Washington, for instance: the Minister, Lord Tremayne, will follow any advice he gives and Rolfe is delighted with the idea."

"I see. A form of power." As Vanin listened, he remembered his own words as he had looked at the photograph in Malendin's office: "He is used to power, but his power comes *through* people rather than over them."

"Yes, power, but only in a sense. I think it is really approval that Rolfe wants. The need to be relied on. I've only been with him for under a year, but I felt it the first day he engaged me. I could almost hear his thoughts: 'This man is a Hungarian refugee. I have been very kind and given him a job. He would find it difficult to get another job. Therefore I know that he will serve me well. He will also be very grateful to me.'"

"Approval, eh?" Vanin suddenly felt comfortable and secure, for he was doing the job he liked doing. He didn't feel like an agent or a spy any more, but just a policeman interviewing a witness.

"It's strange. The man is a scholar, a savant if you like, and they are usually the most independent people in the world. Yet, Martin Rolfe wants influence and he wants approval. Have you reached any conclusions about that, Mr. Arabin?"

"Yes, I think so." Arabin frowned and Vanin could see that the character of his employer fascinated him.

"I think that underneath everything Rolfe is a basically insecure and possibly frightened man. I think that only by holding influence over other people and gaining their approval can he get the sense of security he needs. It's as though every committee he sits on, every report he writes, makes him feel safer: like a very rich man who works twelve hours a day to be richer because he dreads poverty. Every share certificate in his bank, every factory he owns are like barriers shutting off that dread of what will probably never happen.

"That's why I said Rolfe would kill his letter writer, Mr. Vanin. I saw his face when he opened the first one, and it was a killer's face all right. His security is threatened, and that's the one thing he needs in life."

"And just what do you think he is frightened of?" Vanin's policeman's voice showed nothing but polite curiosity.

"I've no idea, but it's something concrete all right. I think that at some time in his life Rolfe may have done something, or had something done to him, and the memory is always with him. He has tried to shut it out with work, with the approval of important people, but it is always there in the back of his mind. Then, one day, he opens a scribbled letter and the terror comes into the light."

"I see." Vanin concentrated for a moment. A man is frightened, he thought. A man of influence who surrounds himself with powerful friends, and sits on committees, and advises governments. But all the time that fear is waiting to come out into the light.

Just what could have caused a fear like that? he wondered. An imaginary childhood terror—a compulsive neurosis that started a long time ago? No, those were the obvious, *doctor's,* solutions, but they didn't fit here. Those scrawled notes pointed to a fear that was real.

A threat of violence, then—of prosecution for some indiscretion of the past? No, nothing like that, for a man like Rolfe would have known how to deal with such threats. Vanin considered the report of the Moscow handwriting experts: "This was written by a very old and feeble person with a mental illness."

But, *in the past* was probably right. Something that happened a long time ago when Rolfe was a boy or a young man. Something which still terrified him. "The Gaunt Woman who can blast you."

Yes, *the Gaunt Woman.* Probably the words didn't refer to a person at all, but a thing. Something that happened years ago, but could still make a very hard, influential economist cry out in terror—the skeleton in the cupboard, the fly in the ointment, the thing in the bricked-up cellar which must never come to light.

"Tell me," said Vanin. "There were four of these letters and, since this last which you gave to us, there appear to have been no more. How is Rolfe now?"

"On the surface he is back to normal, but only on the surface. Underneath I would say he is a very sick man." Arabin picked up the paper that lay on the table. "Look for yourself. This was taken yesterday."

"Thank you." Vanin took the newspaper which Arabin had opened at the financial page. Above the market prices, there were headlines reading, CITY WAITS FOR TREASURY FIGURES, and below the headlines a picture showing the same face he had studied in Malendin's office. Rolfe looked quite different now. The thin, academic features seemed even thinner, and there was no smile in the eyes. He still looked powerful and efficient, but it was a defensive power now: the face of a Prussian general in defeat.

"Yes, I do see," he said, "but tell me something—what do you know about Rolfe's personal life? Has he a family, for instance?"

"No, no family—no children, that is. I seem to have heard there was a child that died a long time ago, but I'm not sure. There is a wife, though—I met her once." Arabin paused for a moment as though the memory was somehow important, lighting another cigarette as he did so.

"It was sometime last winter," he went on. "There were a couple of urgent papers for Rolfe to sign, and I had to drive down to his house one Saturday. . . . That's right. About the end of February it must have been, just after he took me on. He had a house in what they call the Fens, to the north of Cambridge. I remember the drive down well. It's a very flat countryside, with ditches running straight out into the horizon and big churches standing out like ships on every skyline. It was almost dusk when I got to the nearest village, a place called Heronsford. Just a hamlet, really, with a few houses standing round a church and a pub. I stopped for a drink and asked the way. I remember it was very cold, with patches of mist rising up from the empty fields.

"Anyway, I got my directions in the pub, and drove on towards Rolfe's house. It was about four miles from the village, down a narrow lane, and at first sight was just the kind of place I'd expected. There was a high wall running round the grounds, and a porter's lodge with a pair of wrought-iron gates beside it. The porter had to ring through to the house before letting me in.

"But the house itself—that really surprised me. It stood on a little hill which made it tower over the flat countryside, and it was very tall with gables and spires, and every form of architecture going: Victorian Gothic I think they call the style. It looked grotesque in the dusk.

"But this was the strange thing. Rolfe is a rich man in his own right, Chairman of Western Chemicals among other things, yet his house was in terrible repair, all the brickwork needed pointing, and a great line of guttering was hanging loose. It looked as though it hadn't had a workman near it for years.

"Anyway, I went to the door—the paint was peeling from it—and rang the bell, one of those old-fashioned ones worked by wires you pulled. And the maid who opened the door was rather like the house itself. She was a very old woman dressed in a shabby apron which hadn't been washed for weeks. She was bent too, sort of twisted—how do you say it?" He struggled for the right word.

"You mean she was deformed?"

"Yes, that's it, deformed. A cripple, and as I said, very old and dirty. She let me in and told me to wait in the hall while she went to fetch her master.

"And the hall was brown, Mr. Vanin—it was all brown. There was a faded brown carpet on the floor, chipped brown panelling hung with weapons, and ugly brown furniture you couldn't sell for fifty pounds. That was the house of a man who could write a check for half a million any time he wanted to."

"I see. You interest me. And did you meet the wife?"

"No, not really, though I saw her. Rolfe came out and signed the papers. He did it very quickly and, though they were important, I got the feeling that somehow he resented my bringing them. Then, just as I was leaving, I looked up and saw a woman standing at the top of the stairs. I think it must have been Lady Rolfe, because when she called down and asked him how long he'd be, she used the term 'my dear.' . . .

"Yes, that was his wife and, like the house and the servant, she seemed all wrong: an elderly woman, in her sixties probably, but got up like a young girl, with dyed blonde hair and a dress I wouldn't let my daughter wear. Her face could have belonged to a fading street walker. It was dead white, and the make-up stood out like red sealing wax on an envelope."

"But you didn't speak to her?"

"No, Rolfe just let me out, and I've never been in the house since. He has a flat in London and stays there most of the time." Arabin finished his drink and ground out the cigarette. "That's about all I can tell you about his private life, I'm afraid. Rolfe seems to have no vices, and very few interests outside his public work."

"So it seems. All the same, he must have had one vice or one passion in his time; that seems certain. And you don't like him, do you, Mr. Arabin?"

"No, I don't like him." Arabin considered for a moment. "I can't tell you why, though. He's a good enough boss in most ways, but there's something about him—a kind of coldness which, at times, makes you feel you're not with a real person at all. If it wasn't for that, I don't think I'd be talking to you now. Even for the sake of my family, I don't think I would be."

"Is that so, Mr. Arabin? All the same, you are talking to me, so let's have a toast, shall we?" Without asking if he wanted another drink, Vanin got up and refilled their glasses at the bar.

"Yes," Vanin said, returning. "Let's have a toast. That you may see your wife and children again."

"I'll drink to that." Arabin raised his glass, and there was suddenly hope in his face. "Does this mean that you believe my story? That you are going to let them out?"

"No, not yet, I'm afraid. It merely means that I am inclined to believe your story, because I don't think you would make up anything so very unlikely. If I find out that you have spoken the truth and this letter writer exists, then your family will be flown to England on the first available plane. They are ready and waiting now. My department instructed the Hungarian police to hold them in the Belitza prison with their bags packed." He drank his whiskey and set the glass down on the table.

"Yes, if all goes well," he added, "you will see them soon. If, on the other hand, you have been deceiving us, then I'm afraid they may stay in that prison for a very long time." He stood up as he spoke. "Well, goodbye for the time being, Mr. Arabin. And don't worry, I will keep you informed of my progress."

He gave the man a final, prim, and rather old-maidish smile, and without another word walked out of the room.

It was dark now. Dark and cold, with a hint of snow from the east, and the street lamps glowing like oranges in the damp air. Vanin turned up his coat collar and walked forward, looking at the bright shop windows with their messages of seasonal good will and exhortations to buy—just three more days to Christmas and already the decorations looked slightly aged and tawdry; paper masks, green trees, and tinsel dolls almost ready for the dustbin.

And somewhere in this vast, sprawling town was the person he had to find, the man or woman who knew why Martin Rolfe was afraid—the reason for his decayed house, his deformed servant, the wife with that ravaged harlot's face and a dress that Michael Arabin would not allow his daughter to wear.

Arabin. He frowned as he considered the man, for his early words were still like a blow to Vanin—like spittle on his face. "No, you are not animals. . . . You are Russians."

All the same, Arabin had been telling the truth: he was quite certain of that. Somewhere, far back in Rolfe's past, probably a very nasty event had taken place and it was up to him to find what it was. He hadn't much time either. Three days after Christmas Rolfe would leave for Washington and he had to be well in the net before then.

Vanin stopped suddenly and looked at the building in front of him. He had left the shopping areas now, and for some time had been walking among empty, dimly lit office blocks. On the whole dimly lit, that was. The building in front of him was a blaze of light, with floodlamps playing on its towering stories of glass and marble. The sign over the bronze doors read, CENTURY HOUSE, HEADQUARTERS OF WESTERN CHEMICAL INDUSTRIES.

Yes, Rolfe was chairman of that company, Arabin had said, and it didn't fit at all. All this façade of wealth and power linked to a man who wouldn't even paint his own front door. . . . It was time to start work. Vanin crossed the street towards a line of phone booths.

"Gloucester five one, nine one." It was well after business hours, but the office he was calling remained open. It was always open to the right caller.

"Just what can I do for you?" The quiet, anonymous voice at the end of the line couldn't quite conceal its foreign accent.

"Homeway," he said. "Homeway Productions—Extension 8-5." Almost at once the connection went through, and he heard a voice he knew well; a loud, jolly voice that made him feel much less alone.

"Hullo, Gregor," he said. "Yes, Peter Vanin here. How are you, my dear chap? Good, I'm very glad. I saw your sister a few days ago. Her hair appears to be red this year." He heard Gregor Tanek chuckle good-naturedly, and a chair creak as Gregor shifted his enormous bulk to a more comfortable position.

"Yes, I know that Malendin would have told you to help me," Vanin went on, "but I won't trouble your people more than I can help. There are just two things I want from you at the moment. Firstly, I want to know about the girl you sent to meet me in Ireland. . . . That's right, Kate Reilly. . . . I see: she has worked for us for three years, and is quite reliable. Good; that puts my mind at rest on one score." He reached in his pocket and pulled out the scrap of paper that Arabin had given him.

"Now I want you to send off a letter for me, Gregor. The central post offices are still open, I imagine. No, there is nothing to write down. All you need is a plain sheet of paper and an envelope. I want the paper to be well dusted with fuchsin powder. That's right, the stain. . . .

"Sorry, Gregor, but I'm afraid I didn't quite catch that," Vanin said and his voice hardened slightly. "Yes, I know it's late, but you'll just have to find some. This is very important indeed. . . . Good, I knew I could rely on you. Now here is the address. The name is Smith—quite certainly a pseudonym. Yes, J. Smith, Poste Restante Box 5, South Hammersmith G.P.O. . . .

"Thank you, Gregor. Yes, it must be in the post tonight—that's quite essential. Thanks again then, and goodbye for the present."

He replaced the phone and glanced at his watch. It was exactly eight o'clock, and in twelve hours' time, that telltale envelope would be lying in its pigeonhole ready to be collected. To be collected by a person who was said to be mentally ill—a person who had been expecting a letter for several days now and would probably not wait till he got home, but open it in the street or the post office itself. And if that happened—

Vanin smiled to himself and pushed open the door of the phone box. Everything was going smoothly and according to plan. With a little luck, tomorrow would take him just where he wanted to be. Right into the sick mind of the person who knew how to frighten Sir Martin Rolfe.

All the same, he was tired now—terribly tired. He turned and began to walk quickly up the road towards the tube station and his hotel.

CHAPTER IV

It snowed for six hours during the night and at early morning the snow froze. Now it lay over London in a tight, shimmering carpet, very beautiful, but quite impermanent; before evening it would have become a waste of grey, clinging mud.

Kate Reilly stood at a corner of King Street, Hammersmith, looking across at the post office. A small, unimportant building, she was glad to see, merely flattered by the adjective "General." She had been there for a quarter of an hour already, and at any moment the doors were due to open. The mail vans had come and gone from the side entrance, and through the frosted glass windows facing the street she could see figures moving. Vanin had told her to get there just on the hour, but she liked to be early, for she was that kind of girl. Besides, she was very curious. He had rung her at six-thirty with his instructions, but he had told her only what to do and not why. There had been no hint of explanation in that formal, precise voice on the phone. Just instructions and at the end a number, almost grudgingly given, to ring him back to report her progress. Five minutes later she had dialled that number and checked the address: a small, private hotel in Kensington.

But at last the doors were opening. With a sigh of relief, for her feet were like ice, she crossed the road and walked into the office, noting the layout of its counters as she did so: parcels to the right, licences and savings certificates in the centre, stamps and letters on the left. She bought four stamped envelopes and, going to a side table, pulled a writing pad from her bag and began to compose a long and unnecessary letter to a friend. Her position gave her a good view of the door.

But, whatever Peter Vanin might have told her, the person she had to follow didn't seem to be in any hurry. The office was quite busy, but the business was all routine: office boys buying blocks of stamps, withdrawers of savings certificates, housewives laden down with Christmas parcels. There was just one man she watched suspiciously for a moment. A tall, harassed-looking man, who came in muttering angrily to himself as though in extreme annoyance. Then he moved to the counter, parted with thirty-one pounds for National Health contributions, and went out still muttering.

Eight thirty-five. She had finished two letters now, and the clerk behind the licence counter was beginning to eye her with a good deal of curiosity. She ignored him, and tearing out another sheet of paper from her pad, started on a third.

Dear Mary—It seems ages since I heard from you, and hope that everything is— She stopped dead in the middle of the sentence, staring at the door, her pen slipping forward and tearing into the paper.

For this might be it—this might be the person they wanted. She watched the man coming slowly through the doorway and concentrated on the probable description that Vanin had given her. "Certainly old—possibly male—may seem ill, or nervous and jittery."

Yes, this man was old all right. She couldn't see much of the face, for his felt hat was pulled down and a thick, brown muffler covered his mouth. But there was age in that slow, stiff walk towards the counter, and the hint of sickness in that bent body. It was wrapped in a ragged overcoat that made it look like a bundle of brown rags.

But she had nothing to go on yet, nothing at all. All she had was an old man in shabby clothes walking into a post office. It was a poor neighbourhood, and there must be thousands of men looking like him in this area alone. Yet, as he passed her she seemed to sense an atmosphere, an aura, around him which was as strong as a physical smell. She suddenly felt like a book collector bent over an old volume he has never seen listed in a catalogue, who all at once hears a voice saying "Buy me" from the yellow pages. She was almost certain that her first hunch was right, that this was the person whom Vanin wanted her to follow.

The man walked across to the left-hand counter, and leaned against the wire grill. He spoke through his muffler and, though Kate couldn't distinguish the words, from his manner he seemed to be a regular visitor. Without answering him at first, the clerk turned to a row of pigeonholes behind him and pulled out a letter. He grinned slightly as he slid it under the wire. "I hope this is the one you've been expecting," he said.

"Yes, I've been expecting it all right. I've been expecting it for a long time." Through the woolen muffler the voice sounded like something rotten breaking in two. The old man turned away from the counter and stood quite still for a moment, staring at the envelope and balancing it in his hand, as though hoping to judge its contents from the weight and texture. Kate prayed for him to open it.

But he didn't open it—not just then. For perhaps half a minute he held it like that, turning it over and over in an oddly clawlike hand, while Kate watched him with all pretence of letter writing forgotten. Let him just break the flap and she would know what to do, have the sign that Vanin had promised. Transparent powders putting their mark on him and turning red against the moisture of human skin. He pushed the envelope away into the folds of his coat and began to move towards the door.

But she had to be sure. Vanin had told her that his plan was partly a gamble and depended on the man opening the letter in front of her. All she had to go on was a hunch, and this man might be anyone: an old-age pensioner collecting a long-expected present from some distant son or daughter, a boarding-house tenant wishing to conceal his mail from a prying landlady. If she were to follow him now, the person they wanted might come later and she would have failed. She stood by the counter, completely irresolute, and then suddenly her body stiffened and she knew she was right. She was now quite prepared to bet on her hunch; she recognized for certain the aura this man carried. It was not illness or nervousness as Vanin had suggested, but something much simpler—plain anger. For as he pulled back the door his face turned slightly towards hers and she looked at his eyes. A pair of old, tired, and probably feeble eyes, but there was more malice in them than she had ever seen on a human face. She tucked away her pad, dropped the two finished letters into a post box, and followed him out into the street.

It was a long, slow walk. The old man moved carefully across the frozen pavements, as though fearing a fall, pausing for a moment at every corner. In the crowded streets with shops and hurrying pedestrians it wasn't too difficult to follow him, of course, for Kate could stop when he did, and peer into a shop window. But soon they were on the long stretch of arterial road with streams of traffic pouring into London, where there were no shops and the pavements were almost deserted. She kept well behind him, walking very slowly and praying he wouldn't turn round.

They were almost to the river now. The towers of the bridge loomed high above them like fairy-tale castles, and from the opposite bank she could hear a rattle of road drills, very faint and muffled through the frozen air. The man paused before the bridge for a moment, as though uncertain of his way; then he turned right and walked down a flight of steps leading to the towpath.

The tide was very high and the water nearly up to the lip of the embankment. As they walked along the narrow track, a tug swung under the bridge dragging a line of barges and from far downstream Kate heard the distant howl of a ship's siren. The Thames suddenly seemed an unfriendly river the colour of dull lead, with a big oil streak drifting in midstream, and the white flashes of screaming gulls. She kept well in against the wall, following that slow, muffled figure, and all at once she felt more alone than she had been in all her life.

For the man had stopped. He had stopped and pulled something out of his pocket, and he was looking at it. He turned round and started to walk back towards her. Kate crossed to the embankment and lit a cigarette, leaning out over the grey water and watching the tug begin to swing its barges round a bend. In the road above, buses churned through the snow and the road drills sounded like distant gunfire. She was in the heart of London and all around her were commonplace, familiar things; so why was she afraid? Why did she stiffen as those dragging footsteps walked slowly towards her, and feel so completely alone as a brown arm came up and its hand settled on the parapet beside her? Kate worked for one of the toughest organizations in the world, and her training had been thorough. All the same, she suddenly felt like a frightened child as the man looked down at her and she felt his aura as positive as a gas surrounding him.

"Well, young lady, let's have a little talk, shall we? Just why are you following me?" The man's muddy voice brushed aside her protest and, as he spoke, the muffler slipped down to show the face behind it. The face was without scar or blemish, but like something out of a nightmare, a rat's face, stripped of the fur—an old, grey grandfather of the sewers grinning as it started to gnaw its way into a corpse. Kate seemed to see right through the flesh and bone and make out the years of hate and bitterness that had turned that face into the dreadful thing it was.

"Oh yes, you were following me all right. I saw you in the post office, and I came down here just to make sure. Besides, I was half expecting to be followed, you know. Your employer is not an unintelligent man, though it seems I didn't give him enough credit." He lifted his hand and she saw that Vanin's powder had done its job. The fingers were stained a dark, reddish brown.

"Yes, a good idea," the voice went on, "but we can stop playing games now. I would have liked to keep Sir Martin in suspense for a little longer, but it doesn't matter now—no, it doesn't really matter." The smile grew even wider and there was no mistaking the mania behind it.

"And here is what you want, my dear. Here is the thing you are paid to find out—my name and address. How much will you be paid, I wonder? How much can a little secretary girl get for helping such a great man?" A piece of paper was thrust into Kate's hand as he spoke, and at the same time his face began to creep closer to hers. Closer and closer it came, the foul breath like sewer gas around her and the stained fingers tilting her chin upwards. And, as Kate looked into those mad eyes, she knew quite clearly what was going to happen. She also knew that there was nothing to be done about it: no struggle, no running away or calling for help, nothing at all. It was not she but the job that mattered; let her once call out and everything would be finished.

"And now you're going to pay me, my dear," he said. "I want you to be able to tell your master that I was paid for the information he wanted." There was a hand on her shoulder now, but she didn't resist, didn't even try to resist, though it was like the end of the world. She just stood there, still and passive, as the hand tightened, his face touched hers, and slowly and deliberately the grey lips found her mouth.

"Sorry, my dear, I really am very sorry." Peter Vanin listened to Kate's voice on the phone, feeling the nausea in it, and his own voice was very gentle. "Yes, unpleasant things do happen in our job sometimes, but you must accept them, I'm afraid. And I'm very grateful that you didn't resist him; that might have spoiled everything.

"Now, after he kissed you, he just walked off, leaving you with his name and address. Could I have it, please? . . . Thanks—John Flack, 32 Silver Pine Grove, Putney." He made a note in his pocket book. "And don't worry, Kate. Don't worry at all. You'll get over that kiss, but I can promise you one thing; it may take Mr. Flack quite a time to forget what I do to him. Goodbye now, and thanks again."

He replaced the phone and stood quite still for a moment, staring round the empty hall of his hotel. His face showed no emotion at all. Then, as though reaching a sudden decision, he picked up the phone again and started to dial another number. He might be breaking orders, since Malendin had told him to work on his own as much as possible, but he was beginning to feel out of his depth. Very soon he would be dealing with a most unpleasant form of maniac, and he needed a specialist on his side. When he made his next move it would be with reinforcements.

Quiet suburban streets on a quiet winter's evening, with the thawing snow lying in patches on the roofs and the pavements and the small, well-kept gardens. Well-kept houses, too, with paths leading up to them, and sham Tudor timbers on the stucco, and the names of honeymoons above every door—*Tintagel, Napoli, Costa Brava.* Here and there curtains were drawn back from the windows, giving glimpses of Christmas trees and families settled round the fire or television set. A pleasant, respectable neighbourhood, with an air of coziness and warmth and nice people. Men with steady jobs, women with children at private schools, a car in the garage, money in the bank, latticed windows to shut out the cold. And outside, in the cold, a man on his way to keep an appointment.

Peter Vanin walked slowly down Silver Pine Grove, and somehow he seemed to fit into the area; a senior clerk coming home from work to an evening by the fire—books and slippers and children and warm things. There was a slight envy in his eyes as he looked at those well-kept houses, but now and then he smiled as he read the names. A postman's job in England must need a great deal of skill and perseverance, he decided.

Thirty—*Ben Nevis,* thirty-one—*Sans Souci,* thirty-two—No, there was no name by that number, no little glowing lantern in the porch, no air of careful, middle-class prosperity. The garden was choked with weeds, and the privet hedge by the wall had grown into fair-sized trees, reaching the height of the roof and giving the building the appearance of a gigantic mass of vegetation. No chink of light came from the windows, but somehow Vanin knew the house was occupied. It had the feeling of something out of one of Grimm's grimmer fairy stories—a dwelling hidden away in the woods and waiting for a visitor.

He pulled back the rusty gate and walked across the ruin of a garden. The stucco of the house had crumbled before the pressure of the bushes, leaving naked patches of brick-work exposed, and the door looked as though it had not been painted since the house was built. He pressed the switch beside it and, very faintly and far away in the distance, heard a bell ringing.

For a long time Vanin stood there, but no one came. Across the street a familiar scene was being enacted. A shiny car drew up, turned into the drive, and a bowler-hatted man got out and walked quickly and happily towards his front door—his own door which had probably been paid for, like everything else he owned. As the door opened, Vanin saw a woman come forward to kiss him and heard the sound of music and children's laughter.

Once again he pressed the bell, and at last he heard boards creak, and heavy, slow footsteps coming towards him. There was the sound of a bolt being withdrawn, and the rattle of a chain. Then the door opened and he looked at the face of the man he had come all the way from Moscow to see.

And, though he had come prepared for something unpleasant, though Kate had described it to him, Vanin drew back slightly as he looked at the face of John Flack. There was something obscene about it, something horrible in that low, hairless skull with its skin wrinkled like old leather as it joined the sagging features. Something unspeakable in the twisted, malicious mouth, and in the eyes that seemed to glow in the darkness of the hall. As he looked at that face, Vanin felt a sudden pity for Martin Rolfe. Whoever he was, whatever he knew, John Flack would be a very horrible enemy.

"So, my friend has sent another representative, has he?" Like his face, Flack's voice was just as Kate had described it:

thick and muddy and appearing to come from deep down in his body. "Yes, Sir Martin has been very smart, hasn't he? He puts stain on a letter and gets a little girl to follow me. But when I give her the address and he knows where I am, he doesn't come himself. It's strange, that, and I wonder why. Is it that he couldn't come, perhaps—that he was too ill to come?" The voice broke off into a cackle of laughter.

"Mr. Flack, could I come inside and talk to you? It's very cold out here." Vanin forced his face into a smile.

"Yes, of course you can come in, though there's very little to talk about. I'm only talking seriously to the person I addressed my letters to." Flack lowered the chain and pulled open the door.

"Welcome to my castle," he said. "But don't try anything—just be very careful. I may be an old man, but I'm quite ready for you." He raised his hand to show what it held: a big, heavy revolver, slightly reminiscent of a Frontier Colt. In his time Vanin had made a study of guns, and he recognized it, a forty-five calibre Webley—British Officers' Standard Pattern—First World War Issue.

"No, I won't try anything," Vanin said, smiling at the revolver. "Not while you're holding that." He walked past Flack into the house, smelling the mustiness of it that came from old books, and rotting timber, and years of neglect. There was also another, chemical, smell which Vanin seemed to remember but couldn't quite place.

"In here, please." Flack pulled back another door on the right of the hall and motioned him through. As Vanin entered the room, he stood quite still for a moment staring around him, for it was like something out of a nightmare. A big, rather graceful room, probably designed as a parlour, but its builder wouldn't have liked it now. Instead of curtains, sacking covered the windows, and dust and cobwebs lay everywhere. An old-fashioned oil heater glowed dully in the grate, and all over the floor there were books—hundreds of books. Some of them lay in shelves, some were spread out on the table, but most of them were piled on the worn linoleum; one or two of the piles nearly reached to the ceiling. As they walked forward, Vanin saw a mouse regarding him gravely, completely without fear, from behind a large, leatherbound volume.

But it wasn't the books, or the dirt, or the old, broken furniture that interested him; it was the walls—the walls and the pictures on them. Pictures cut from newspapers and magazines and pasted roughly onto the plaster, pictures of just one subject. From every corner of the big, dusty room the face of Martin Rolfe seemed to be watching him.

"No, your employer can't say I neglect him, can he?" Mack waved Vanin to the one chair that the room possessed and stood with his back to the smoking oil stove. He still kept the revolver in his hand. "Now let's get down to facts, shall we, Mr.—thank you—Mr. Vanin. Just what message did Rolfe tell you to give me?"

Vanin didn't answer for a moment. Very slowly, to gain time, he pulled off his gloves and laid them on the arm of the chair. He had to consider carefully before he made a move. His first plan had been to pose as a representative of Rolfe's, but that wouldn't work now. Every line of that sagging, ratlike face told him it wouldn't work.

"There's no message, Mr. Flack," he said. "There couldn't be a message, because I haven't come from Rolfe, you see. Like you I am an enemy of Rolfe's, and I work for quite a different organization."

"I see. Then you'd better start to tell me about it, Mr. Vanin. You'd better tell me quickly." The gun began to come up as he spoke. "Just who are you, and who do you work for?"

"That doesn't matter." Vanin leaned forward, ignoring the gun. "All you need to know is that we are people who can pay you—pay you well." He reached in his pocket and pulled out his wallet. The ridge of notes showed like a blue tongue against the leather. "We know that you have certain information about Rolfe, and I have come to buy it from you."

"So, that's it." Once again Flack gave that short cackle of

laughter that had nothing to do with humour. "No, you can put away your money, I have nothing to sell you. My information is very private and I need it all for my own use. Now, just how did you find out about it, and what do you know about me?"

"We know nothing about you personally, Mr. Flack, except that you are a man who can help us. All we know is that, during the last few weeks, Martin Rolfe has been receiving letters from you and he is very, very frightened by those letters. The first one was enough to give him a minor heart attack." He saw a glow of satisfaction light up the man's face as he spoke.

"Well, it doesn't matter how, but we managed to intercept one of those letters, and I have traced you through it. Now I want to talk business. We want to buy a share of this information which could give a man like Rolfe a heart attack. We want to know what is the thing you refer to as the Gaunt Woman."

"The thing—you say the thing!" This time Flack's laugh was quite genuine: a great, convulsive belch of laughter that echoed around the room. "You don't really know anything, do you, Mr. Vanin? You call her a thing." He laid the gun down on a table and leaned back against the mantelpiece with his arms stretched out behind him. There was an oddly crucified look about the posture of his body, as though nails were holding it in position.

"The Gaunt Woman is not a thing, my friend, but a person—a sort of person, that is. She was born on Christmas Eve exactly twenty years ago, and she died the same day. Only a few people ever saw her, and she was soon forgotten; even I forgot her. Then one evening when I was sitting in this room, I looked at a picture in a magazine and I saw her ghost. And as I saw it I knew that I held the great Sir Martin Rolfe in the hollow of my hand. And that's the only clue I'm going to give you, Mr. Vanin. The rest of the story you can discover for yourself."

In the hollow of my hand! As he listened, Vanin suddenly remembered Malendin's use of exactly the same phrase. He looked at the man's evil, but not entirely mad, face and slowly pushed the wallet away, for he knew what he was dealing with. Flack didn't want money from him. Flack didn't want anything except the infliction of pain. His first attack had failed, it seemed, and those reinforcements would be needed. Somehow Flack would be made to talk, but that wasn't Vanin's job any more. Even the department wouldn't want that, for it believed in specialists for such work. Outside in the quiet, respectable street one of those specialists would be waiting now and it was he who would find out the story of the Gaunt Woman. All the same, there was one thing Vanin wanted to know before he handed over.

"Tell me something," he said. "Just what did Rolfe do to make you hate him so much?"

"He didn't do anything. He just succeeded—like I would have *succeeded,* if they'd given me the chance." There was a strange accentuation of the word, and in the man's face Vanin saw years of pain and emptiness and hate which had grown to mania. Mania which made him hunt magazines and newspapers for pictures of his enemy and paste them on walls to keep the hate fresh and healthy.

"Succeeded? I'm afraid I don't understand you."

"No, you won't understand; nobody ever understands—nobody even tries to." The words were like an often repeated litany, and Vanin could imagine him muttering them to himself over and over again.

"But try and understand, Mr. Vanin. Try and think what it feels like to know that you should have got on—should have come to the top—but always stayed in the gutter. . . . Oh, yes, I know them, the people who succeed—the people like Rolfe. At school and university with their nice manners and accents to please the teachers and dons. Not working any harder than I did, no brighter than I was, but always coming to the top; always getting the Alpha Plus when I had the Beta Minus." The words rambled on like a prayer to the great god whose name was Hatred.

"And afterwards—in business. Always the same people

fighting to the top and not caring who they trampled on in their way. 'Fetch this, Flack— You'll have to stay and work late tonight, Flack— Take your wages and get out.' Then they ride home to their women in big flashy cars while I wait in the gutter.

"Yes, their women!" His tongue ran over his grey lips as he spoke the word. "They always have the best women. Women worship success, and they take their pick. I had a woman once, you know. For ten years I was married to her, all happy and secure, till one of them kicked me out of my job and she left me. Went off with a more successful man who could support her properly, the bitch said.

"A good man too, she says he is. Allows me to live in my house he does—his house of course, since he paid off my debts and took over the mortgage. I'd have hated the bastard less if he hadn't done that."

"I think I'm beginning to understand you," Vanin said slowly. He saw suddenly that though Flack had failed in everything, he would have been a great success in other ages and countries. With his two virtues of hate and envy he would have made an excellent Christian persecutor, witch hunter, and Jew baiter. "I know how you feel. Your own life has gone wrong, so you hate people who have been more successful. But why Rolfe in particular?"

"No, you still don't understand. I don't hate Rolfe in particular, but he's one of them; one little tin soldier in that huge army of the successful; one of the people who kept me down." The beads of sweat on Flack's forehead looked slightly indecent—a disease against the wrinkled skin. "But I dreamed of getting one of them, you know. For years I dreamed about it. Just the thought of getting one of those little gold and silver soldiers in my power and making him squirm. . . .

"And sometimes dreams come true don't they? Mine did. One day I saw a certain picture and it told me something about Sir Martin Rolfe—something which could break him. I may be a failure, Mr. Vanin, but I'm not a fool. I put two and two together and I made certain enquiries. Now there is one little gold soldier safe in my box with the lid closed down on him. And when he comes out, he'll be mad, you know—as mad as you probably think I am." He smiled suddenly with the terrible sanity of the insane.

"I don't think you're mad, Mr. Flack." Vanin forced the disgust out of his voice. He remembered what had happened to Kate, and there was nothing he would have liked better than to pull out his little pen gun and put a bullet through Flack's forehead. He wasn't paid to do that, though. For the time being, at least, he was paid to be nice to Flack. He suddenly hated his job.

"No, you're not mad," he repeated. "But neither am I one of your army of the successful. So can't we do business and help each other? As I said, I'm prepared to pay well for your information." This was Vanin's last appeal, and if it failed he would hand over to someone else. In a way he hoped that Flack wouldn't take it.

Flack didn't take it. He straightened from the mantelpiece and picked up the gun, toying with it in his hand.

"No," he said. "We can't do business, and I don't want your money. As this room may show you, I have a job. I deal in secondhand books. A runner, they call it, the lowest form of life in the trade. Still, by bringing goods to the more successful, I make a little money. Enough to allow me to eat and indulge in my rather childish hobby. You might be able to guess what it is, Mr. Vanin. I play with toy soldiers. Little gold and silver soldiers who know how to die well." He reached into his jacket and held out something in his left hand—a knight in armour that glittered strangely as though with a life of its own. Then he pushed it back into the musty prison of his pocket.

"And now, Mr. Vanin, I want you to leave me alone—I've said all I'm going to say. And don't come back, either." He'd stopped playing with the gun now, and it was pointing at Vanin's heart. "The information I have is my own, and I'm not selling it to anyone. But if you really hate Rolfe, don't worry about him any more. When I've finished with him, Sir Martin Rolfe will be dead—dead or insane."

Flack turned and walked towards the door. Following him, Vanin glanced back at the gloves he had left lying on the chair. A nice pair of leather gloves, looking quite innocent on the worn cloth. To Vanin they were not just gloves, however, but a key. A key that would open the door to his reinforcements.

"Good night," he said, and without another word stepped out into the dark.

CHAPTER V

The man that Gregor Tanek had sent stood at the corner of the road and there was no mistaking him. As had been arranged, his fawn-coloured overcoat was open to show a bow tie and his trilby had a little feather set jauntily in the band. There was a briefcase in his left hand, and his right toyed with a cigarette case. He was very beautiful and smelled strongly of scent.

"Ah, good evening, old boy." He responded to Vanin's curt nod with a beaming smile that lit up his whole face, and fell into step beside him. There was a certain grace in his walk, a smooth rotundity of movement that a woman might have envied. "Well, do we go to work straight away or may I have a little briefing first?"

Vanin winced slightly as he listened to the man's voice; he was almost sure he could recognize the accent. *"Sie sind Deutsch?"* he said quietly.

"Am I German?" The man raised his eyebrows slightly. "Good Heavens no, old chap. British—British as the flag, though I was born under a bluer sky than usually surrounds these islands. I'm South African Dutch by birth, a Boer, as some people are pleased to call us. And my Christian name is Julius, by the way. My poor dear father had a great passion for Roman history. The other name doesn't matter, does it?"

"No, the surname never matters, and naturally we talk first." Vanin withdrew his arm hurriedly as the man's fingers touched his sleeve to steer him across the road, as though he were a short-sighted old lady.

"Good. Then let's do it in comfort, shall we? On my way here I happened to notice a little eating place round the corner. Nothing grand, but it looked quiet and comfortable enough. As it happens, I'm just longing for a cup of coffee." There was a slight gleam in Julius' eyes as he hurried forward.

The café stood at the very end of Silver Pine Grove, where suburbia proper meets the main road and dies. As Julius had said, it was very quiet; empty in fact, except for a single waitress who looked as if her sole ambition in life was to sleep. Julius beamed as she placed the cups in front of them, and then shook his head sadly over the half-empty sugar basin.

"I wonder, my dear," he said, "if you'd be very, very kind and fill this up for us. I do so like a really sweet drink. . . . Oh, thank you—thank you very much indeed."

He shovelled four spoonfuls into his cup and stirred it to a thick syrup, grinning as he did so. His hand was rather unpleasant, Vanin thought—the middle fingers were of equal length.

"I'm afraid I've got a terribly sweet tooth," Julius said. His age could have been anything between thirty and forty, but his face was white and unlined, a pallid wax tablet on which the years had not written a single word. A face that could be capable of anything or nothing.

"And now should we get down to the sordid details? Your colleagues are always so cagey, and they told me nothing on the phone. They merely said I was to meet you here, wearing these clothes and juggling my cigarette case in a rather ridiculous manner. All I really did gather was that we have to make a man sing."

"Sing?" Vanin frowned and shook his head. "I'm sorry, but I'm afraid I don't understand."

"Oh, dear! How very stupid of me." Julius raised his hands in self-depreciation. "Your English is so good, old chap, that I keep forgetting you are a foreigner. To 'make a person sing' is a term used largely by the British criminal classes—and writers of detective fiction. It means to make him talk—give evidence—spill the beans— Oh, dear! There I go again."

"That's all right, I know what you mean now." Vanin waved aside the cigarettes his companion offered. They were Egyptian and had little green bands round the mouthpieces. "The position is this. There is a man in the house I came out of who has certain information my department needs. I have been unable to get it by normal methods, so I have asked for your help. Your job is to put him into the right frame of mind to give me that information. How you go about it is none of my business, but I was told you are efficient."

"Oh, don't worry about that. I'm efficient all right and I've had very thorough training. Your people wouldn't pay me a very generous retainer if I weren't. All the same, I'm not a miracle worker, and I need certain information. If this chap of yours is to break, I've got to know something about him. People react to different stimuli, you see. What may be intolerable to one man means nothing to another. Tell me about this fellow: age, character, medical history and so on."

He listened to Vanin's description of John Flack, and shook his head sadly.

"A nut case, eh, with a deep hatred of people he considers more successful than himself. Probably a psychopath, I should say, and they are always the most difficult subjects to deal with—a real passion for martyrdom at times, poor lambs. . . .

"And old too! Old and rather decayed. Dear me, this is going to be very difficult. Physical pain would be very little use and might kill him before he spoke a word." There was a sudden sadness in that smooth pale face, and Vanin saw that Julius enjoyed his job. "No, I'll just have to rely on drugs, and I don't like that—I don't like it at all. It's always such a gamble."

"A gamble? But I thought—"

"Oh, yes, you thought that they were all proved, and tried out, and a hundred percent reliable, didn't you? Well, you are quite right, old boy, but only when a great deal of patient research has gone before—when the person in question has been thoroughly examined both physically and mentally. The drug merely lowers the powers of resistance, and then we have to persuade the subject that he wants to talk—that it is in his own best interest to talk. You're asking me to treat a complete stranger almost on the spur of the moment." Julius shook his head, as though pitying the ignorance of all laymen.

"He's alone in the house, you say. Good, that's something in our favour at least. And you left your gloves behind, as an excuse for going back: very thoughtful." He might have been complimenting a child on some slight show of intelligence.

"But he has a gun—how very trying of him. Nobody can say we're overpaid, and I do so hate physical violence. All the same, we are paid, so we'll just have to do our best." He opened his case and transferred two objects into a pocket. Then he handed the case to Vanin.

"You'd better take this, if you don't mind, old boy. I'll be needing my hands free when the time comes." He stood up and looked sadly round the warm little café. "Ah, Duty," he said. " 'Duty, stern daughter of the voice of God.' "

But for all his effeminate, pretentious manner, Julius was efficient, and he knew his job. As Vanin stood back in the shadow of the hedge watching him, he saw efficiency in that quiet, unhurried walk up to the house, in the relaxed body, in the gloved hands hanging loosely at his side, the hands of an expert about to perform a task he understood perfectly. John Flack might have a dozen guns, but he wouldn't stand a chance.

It was over quickly too; so quickly that Vanin could hardly make out the details. He saw the door drag back a little against the chain, saw Flack's face peering out, and, at the same moment, saw something happen to Flack's face. What looked like a black animal appeared to leap out of Julius' hand and attach itself there, while his other hand came up with a thin steel bar in it. The noise of splintering wood was like a little sigh, and then the door fell open. Vanin gave a final glance along the street and walked up the path to the house.

"Well, so far, so good." Julius grinned and bolted the door. "And now, perhaps I'd better release our friend before his lungs are past repair." He bent down towards Flack. The man was crawling on the floor, as though in extreme agony, but he didn't make any noise. His hands were tearing at an obscene black mass that clung to his face like a leech.

"Yes, we'll have you all nice and comfortable in a moment, old chap, but first we must protect our own interests." Julius kicked the gun to one side and tied Flack's wrists together with a length of wire, leaving an end loose. Then he reached for the black thing over Flack's face. It came away with a loud sucking sound, and the flesh behind it was a bright, mottled scarlet. The repulsive mouth was wide open, dragging in great gulps of air, and the eyes were glazed like marbles.

"Now don't worry, my dear. You'll be quite all right in a moment—right as rain." He held up the thing in his hand and smiled at Vanin.

"Neat, isn't it? My own invention and I'm rather proud of it. A plastic mask fitted with a vacuum bottle. Sticks to anything it touches like a limpet, and is almost impossible to take off unless you know where the valve is. The pain is very considerable, of course, and one has to be careful. Just a little too much suction and the lungs would be pulled apart. And that would be most unfortunate, wouldn't it? . . . Ah, so you've recovered, have you? I must say you're no beauty either."

Julius dragged Flack to his feet and neatly pasted a strip of plaster across his mouth. "No, it would never do to disturb the neighbours at this time of night. . . . Now, where shall we take him? I want a couch or a sofa of some kind. Even a table would do at a pinch. In here, perhaps." He nodded at a closed door in the hall beside him.

"No, I don't think that's much use," said Vanin. He remembered the piles of books that almost filled that room. "Let's try this one." He opened the opposite door and pressed the electric switch beside it.

"Well, well," Vanin said, and there was a great curiosity in his eyes. "He really does play with soldiers."

The room was completely bare with naked plaster walls. Its windows had been bricked up and replaced by air vents, and the floor was concrete. The general effect was of a military bunker, but that was not the interesting thing about it. The interest lay in the tables and the glittering figures on them. Four long iron tables stood in two lines, and every table supported a battlefield, with soldiers that seemed to glow with a strange, unearthly light that wasn't just a reflection from the unshaded lamp in the ceiling. Greeks at Marathon with fire on their shields—a Waterloo square standing in burning uniforms before shining French cavalry—a Roman cohort glittering as it marched. John Flack's hobby was a novel one, at least; he didn't merely play with soldiers, he gave them life too—glowing light. Toys of victory for a man who only believed in defeat. It would have been funny if it weren't so horrible.

"Yes, I think this will do us very well." Julius ran his hand across the nearest table, and the armies of Gettysburg fell in heaps to the floor. Then, as easily as lifting a child he swung Flack onto the table and secured his wrists to the top of the table legs.

"Very significant, isn't it?" he went on. "Our friend feels embittered because of failure, so he plays with soldiers. Even makes his room look like part of a fortress. Probably imagines himself to be Caesar or Napoleon from time to time. Very typical and gives us a good picture of his character.

"Rather a dangerous hobby though, I think. This lighting effect puzzles me a little. I wonder if he has produced some form of artificial phosphorescence which he paints on his toys to make them glow." Julius picked up the tiny figure of a Confederate horseman and sniffed at it, looking at the bench by the wall as he did so. On it stood a big glass jar filled with water covering a number of lemon-coloured objects the size and shape of small cigars.

"Yes, he has indeed, the clever old devil. That's yellow phosphorus, all right, and it's one of the most unpleasant substances known. Quite safe when diluted or kept under water, of course, but expose it to air and you get a very nasty reaction." He shook his little finger at the bound body on the table. "You really should be more careful, old chap," he said and took the bag from Vanin and pulled out a bottle and a hypodermic syringe. "And now I think you'd better leave me alone with him for a bit. Sorry to kick you out, but a third person in the room might distract our friend. And though you're probably a good materialist, you might say a little prayer for me. When I've given him his shots, one of three things is going to happen. It may not take at all, and we'll have to try another method. It may work, and he'll be as co-operative as a lamb. Finally, it may drive him right round the bend, and we'll get nothing from him. Just wish me luck and pray that *that* doesn't happen."

He watched Vanin go out and close the door behind him; then he opened his bottle. There was an odd look in his eyes as he started to fill the syringe—a professional and strangely proud look. He might have been a surgeon preparing to save a child's life.

The next part wasn't long, but it seemed like hours to Vanin, standing in the hall, with the atmosphere of the house all around him like a physical thing and his body feeling as cold as death. In a few minutes, if the man who called himself Julius knew his trade, Vanin would learn Flack's secret, but there would be no triumph or pleasure in it. He was paid to do a job, and he would do it to the best of his ability, but he hated the job now. The thought of Flack's ratlike mouth reaching for Kate's lips, and of Julius with his torturer's hands had killed all pleasure. He even felt a slight pity for Sir Martin Rolfe; whatever the man had done, he was the victim of a monster. At the moment Vanin had just one ambition in life—to get out of that mouldering, decayed house and walk among normal people, whatever their jobs or politics. A little clock ticked noisily on the wall above him, and a mouse ran across the floor. Now and again he heard the voice of Julius through the door: a very firm, but quite impersonal voice, which seemed to have lost all trace of individuality. Then the voice stopped, feet came towards him, and the door opened.

"Well, did the stuff work? Will he talk?"

"Yes, I think so, but I'm not sure. I want him to have a few minutes on his own before I start asking questions." Julius lit a cigarette and inhaled deeply, like a man who has just finished a hard piece of work.

"No, I'm not certain how he's going to react, and I was right, you know. Mr. Flack is a psychopath, and we can never tell which way they'll go. I've already given him nearly double the normal first dose as it is—almost enough to kill him, in fact. And that reminds me—" he raised his eyebrows slightly—"if you get what you want, do we have to kill him?"

"Yes, we have to kill him." There was no expression on Vanin's face. "You have to kill him, that is. As you told me, you are paid for it."

"Oh, very well, old boy, I was just enquiring, not complaining. Now just what do you want me to ask him?" He grinned at Vanin's frown and shook his head. "No, I'm sorry, but I'll have to do the talking. That's quite essential, if we're going to get anything out of him at all. After all, we must go by the book, mustn't we?"

"Very well." Though Vanin hated confiding in this man, the answer was something he appreciated and understood. "Flack has some sort of hold on a senior advisor to the British government named Martin Rolfe. He has been writing him letters which at first seemed to be preparations for a blackmail attempt but now appear to have been sent for personal spite. Whatever the motive, however, Rolfe has been terrified by them, and it is my job to find out what Flack's hold over him is. The only clue we have so far is something he refers to as the Gaunt Woman."

"The Gaunt Woman! How very romantic of him. Very well, let's see what he will tell us. Stand in the doorway, will you, and don't make any noise at all." Julius glanced at his watch and walked back into the room.

John Flack still lay on the table, but his face looked quite different. All the hate seemed to have been drained out of it, and only hate had given it life and character. It was a dead, vacant face now, the rather unpleasant mask of a puppet. Mr. Punch lying in his box and waiting for somebody to pull the string. The plaster had been removed from his mouth, but the wire still held his wrists.

"All right, old chap, here we go again." Julius stood beside the table, but he didn't look at Flack. He seemed to take care not to look at him. A few feet away from them the armies of Waterloo glowed like stars.

"Now you know who I am, John, don't you? You know that I am your friend and I have come here to help you—only to help you."

"To help me! Yes, that is right. You said you would help me." Like his face, Flack's voice was completely dead and expressionless: a sound like air being pumped through the body of a corpse.

"Yes, I'm your friend, John, and you must trust me. You must tell me something so that I can help you." Julius' voice hardened slightly. "Just what is it that you know about a man named Martin Rolfe?"

"Rolfe—Martin Rolfe. Yes, I know about him. He's the one I got, and I'm going—I'm going to break him."

"Yes, that's right, you want to ruin him, don't you? People have treated you very badly in life, John, and now you can get your own back at last. You know something about Martin Rolfe and you can break him. Now, tell me about it, John. I'm your friend, so tell me what you know about Rolfe."

"I can destroy him, I can break him—any time I want to." The mouth creased a little as Flack spoke, and there was something horrible in the sight of that dead face smiling.

"Yes, I know that, John, but tell me how. Just how can you break him?"

"Because I've got a good memory. I saw a picture and I recognized her at last. More than twenty years ago it must have been, but I never realized the truth then. It all seemed so obvious at the time, because she'd done it twice before. She was standing outside that shop window, and it was snowing—snowing hard it was, and it's difficult to make out details in the snow. Very tall, she looked—very tall and thin with hair like—"

"Go on, John. Go on and tell me. Just what was her hair like?"

"It was like—like the things I saw in that picture. No, it's so long ago, and I can't describe it—I just can't remember."

"But you must remember, John. You have to remember, because I'm your friend, and I want to help you. I can't help you unless you tell me the truth." Julius still looked away from him, but there was a sudden urgency in his voice.

"Go on now," he said. "A long time ago you saw someone standing outside a shop window. It was snowing heavily and you couldn't see her too well, though. Later on you recognized that person from a picture: a person who has something to do with Martin Rolfe. Well, who is she, John? Is she the person you called the Gaunt Woman?" Julius brought his hand down with a crash on the table.

"Tell me now, John. Just who is the Gaunt Woman?"

"The Gaunt Wooo—" The word broke off as though Flack had been gagged and, at the same moment and without any warning, his face came alive again and it happened. From where he stood Vanin saw every detail, but he had no time to act, only to call out.

"Julius," he cried. "Look out, Julius!" But it was too late. Julius had his face turned away from Flack, and he never saw the sudden light in those mad eyes, or the body starting to swing towards him. Flack's knees caught him in the small of his back and he fell sideways, cannoning against the bench as he did so. The glass jar dropped to the floor and broke. A heap of little cigar-shaped objects lay beside him on the concrete.

It was only seconds but it felt like a year. Vanin hurled himself forwards, but it was to Flack, not Julius, that he went. Julius was unimportant now. He had made a mistake and would just have to look after himself.

But Flack was still important. Flack was the one person in the case who mattered; without him, they might never learn the secret of Sir Martin Rolfe. Vanin's fingers tore madly at the wire that held Flack to the table and, as he did so, he heard a little crackling noise like tearing paper and smelled burnt garlic. He knew exactly what was going to happen, and he strained still harder at the wire, as the crackle grew to a roar and smell thickened into white vapour.

A moment later the wire broke, but it was too late. The bench, half the room, and the man called Julius were a mass of flame.

Five miles away from Flack's house there was an office whose windows were tightly closed. They were always closed after dusk, for the occupant at the office distrusted the treacherous night air. Thick curtains covered them to cut out the merest suspicion of a draught, and at the other side of the room an enormous coke stove glowed in the grate. There was also an electric fire working at full capacity by the desk. The room was like something out of Dante's Inferno, but to General Charles Kirk, head of Her Majesty's Foreign Intelligence Service, it was a near approach to heaven. Smiling like a well-fed cat, he laid down the cigar with which he had been thickening the already overpowering atmosphere, and nodded slightly.

"Yes, Igor," he said. "You've done very well, haven't you?—very well indeed. Let me be the first to congratulate you."

"Thank you, sir." The man across the desk was tall, stooping, and completely hairless. His dark suit was dandified and there was a bright flower in his buttonhole. His bored, slightly vacant expression gave him the air of a well-bred *rentier,* but the air was false. He worked very hard for his living and he had been born in a Paris slum. His name was Igor Trubenoff, chief of the department dealing with Soviet Russia, and at the moment, a very self-satisfied man.

"Yes, things are going very nicely on the whole. We've got that rendezvous at Kerry in Southern Ireland completely tied up now. Nobody can go in or out without our full knowledge."

"Yes, so you've told me many times, Igor, with a great deal of pride. As I've said, I'm pleased with you. Now I suppose we'll just have to wait, and hope that before long a little mouse will come creeping in between our paws." Kirk's right hand, which lacked three fingers, drummed quietly on the desk as he spoke.

"No, General, as it happens, we don't have to wait. The mouse has already arrived. He was landed from one of their trawlers yesterday morning. Here's my first report on him." Trubenoff slid a typewritten folio across the desk.

"Thank you, Igor. I see, a man called Vanin—Peter Vanin. Yes, this is beginning to interest me slightly." His heavy, well-bred features showed no expression as he read down the page.

"Strange, isn't it, Igor?" he said as he pushed the report away from him. "This Vanin seems to be quite an important man, so why should they send him over here now? They had quite a nasty jolt over that Lonsdale affair and have been lying low recently. Why should they risk a man like this Vanin now?" Once again Kirk looked at the paper.

"Yes, educated at the Leningrad Police Academy—attached to the embassy over here in '41—chief—yes, *chief* Soviet adviser to the Hungarian secret police after the uprising. No, Mr. Peter Vanin isn't one of their usual hair-brained fanatics, but a professional, very like ourselves. Something pretty important must have sent him over. I'd very much like to know what our friend Colonel Malendin is up to this time." He leaned back in his chair and pulled hard on the cigar. Then he pointed it at Trubenoff like a weapon.

"Well, Igor, let's have the rest of the story, shall we?—all the rest. The information here has probably been in our files for years. Just cut out the secretive Slav act, and tell me everything you've learned about this Vanin."

"Very well, General, if I must, I must. I was hoping to keep it to myself till I had much more detail." Rather sadly, the Russian leaned forward towards the intercom.

"With your permission," he said, and pressed the switch. A moment later the door opened, and the girl whom Vanin knew as Kate Reilly came into the room.

CHAPTER VI

Vanin knew little about the properties of phosphorus, and when the fire came it was like nothing he had imagined, or even thought possible. A great, hissing, roaring fire, with showers of sparks cracking out across the room, and white tongues of flame licking through the dense garlic vapour. The man called Julius must have died in seconds.

But Flack was dead too; that was the important thing. That last, convulsive movement towards Julius had been too much for the drugged body, and the old, tired heart had stopped beating. Vanin dragged him out into the passage and looked down at the body. It didn't resemble a human being at all; the dead never do. It was like a bundle of rags with a mask stuck on top of them, a bale of rubbish waiting to be cleared away. As Vanin stood staring at it, a wave of flame came belching out across the floor towards him, and Vanin hurled back the door. He didn't know how long phosphorus would burn, but the walls, ceiling and floor were concrete. Also there were no windows to attract inquisitive neighbours. He reckoned he had ten minutes at the outside.

Very quickly he knelt down beside the body and forced himself to tilt back the head and reach into the folds of the jacket. Flack was finished, and Flack was the one he had come all the way from Moscow to find. Only Flack knew the secret of the Gaunt Woman, whatever she might be, and the odds were piling up against Vanin. All the same, he wasn't finished yet. Flack might be dead, but it was still up to Vanin to try and find the information they needed. The department didn't accept failure, and he was as expendable as Julius. Also he was a married man and he had to go on. His fingers ran through every pocket of Flack's clothes, finding nothing at all; then he got up and moved across the passage. Already the paint on the door was starting to blister, and the odour of burning wood was mingling with the garlic smell.

The room in the front of the house, where he had talked to Flack, seemed much darker now. Probably Vanin's eyes were suffering from the fumes, for the piles of books looked oddly unreal: heaped bricks and stones ready for the builders. He stood in the doorway for a moment, hearing the rustle of terrified mice under his feet and seeing the pictures of Martin Rolfe staring down at him. Then he walked across to the desk by the window. The boards beneath him felt soft and rotten, as though they would give way at any moment.

The desk was locked, but he opened it in seconds, his knife sliding in against the catch, and the top rolling back to show the litter of books and papers it contained. Letters and accounts and sale catalogues marked in Flack's spidery hand—nothing to tell Vanin what he had to know.

But all the same, they told him a good deal about Flack's livelihood. A *runner* was the word he had used: the lowest form of life in the secondhand book trade; one who bought from a dealer in the hope of selling quickly to another for a few shillings' profit. As Vanin read through the papers, he heard a crash of falling plaster from the next room.

But there was nothing to help him—not yet. Nothing to tell him what had been Flack's hold over Rolfe: the thing that had made a very powerful man tremble before a scrawled note and a drawing that might have been done by a child. A man who, as Arabin said, needed security. "It's as though every committee he sits on, every report he writes, makes him feel safer."

But there, at last, there might be something. Under the letters and the records of little, unimportant transactions—*buy for seven shillings, sell for ten*—there was a small, flattish book bound in leather. The author's name had been pasted over, but the title stood out clear on the spine and cover: *A Short History of the Devil.*

Vanin opened it, and then suddenly he stiffened, for he knew he was on the way home at last. The book contained no text, for John Flack had removed the pages and very carefully sewn in fresh sheets. Like the walls of his room, they were pasted with cuttings from newspapers and magazines. Not pictures, but the text this time: a complete record of the man he had set out to destroy.

Peter Vanin leafed quickly through that book, and at every page he turned he heard the sound of the fire increasing. The cuttings were in no chronological order, and seemed to have been put in batches. Some were old and yellowed, and some were obviously recent. Most of the earlier ones were photostats copied from newspaper libraries. As he glanced through them, he saw the growth of Rolfe's career: APPOINTMENT OF NEW PROFESSOR—STATEMENT OF TREASURY ADVISER.

But here, almost in the middle of the book, there was something that had nothing to do with Rolfe as a public figure. Three browned and wrinkled columns, with a single heading and a date. Vanin suddenly remembered Flack's own words to him: "The Gaunt Woman was born on Christmas Eve exactly twenty years ago, and she died the same day." The date above the columns was December 29, 1940, and the heading ran: CHRISTMAS MURDER—CHILD KILLER STRIKES AGAIN.

Yes, he had been right when he had looked at Rolfe's picture in Malendin's office. The man's face had seemed to hint at some personal tragedy then, and here was the tragedy looking out at him from twenty years ago. The story was quite clear in front of him. The last night before Christmas, with snow falling; a nursemaid wheeling a pram down a busy street. And she had left the pram for a moment. She had remembered some final card or present and gone into a store, leaving the pram and the baby outside on the pavement—the month-old baby of a senior civil servant named Martin Rolfe.

Then somebody had walked down the street and looked into that pram. Somebody had smiled probably, and wiggled her fingers at the baby, and cooed to it. Then, with a casual look through the shop window, that person had released the brake, and wheeled the pram away through the Christmas crowds. A person who had already killed twice before.

But what about it? Rolfe had had a tragedy in his life. His child had been killed by a maniac, but how did that give Flack power over him? Rolfe was an object of pity, not of shame. With another crash of plaster from the room beyond and smoke drifting in across the passage, Vanin turned the page and saw the first and only picture in the book. It showed a woman about to step into a car, her hands covering her face. There were policemen on either side of her and, behind the police, a crowd of people, shouting and shaking their fists, ELSIE GRANT GUILTY BUT INSANE, ran the headlines above it, LIFE FOR TRIPLE MURDERESS.

Vanin held the book up to the dim light, and skimmed the account of the trial. It was fully reported, and there seemed no doubt as to the woman's guilt. Her husband had left her, and her own child had been killed in a motor accident. She had had a breakdown and was a voluntary patient in a mental hospital but had come home for a week at Christmas. And during that week a little spark of mania or resentment had started to burn in her mind, and three children had died. They had all died in the same way: suffocation—with her fingerprints clear and damning on the pram handles. She had even admitted to what she had done.

No, there was no mystery there, but all the same Vanin now read more carefully. It was his job to be sure of everything. Even with waves of heat spreading across the passage, he had to read on. He read the evidence of the nursemaid, who had been helped, sobbing, into the witness box. He read the medical evidence and the statement of the police, represented by somebody named Detective Inspector George Pode. He started to read the evidence of a witness who claimed to have seen Grant wheel the pram away— Suddenly Vanin stiffened.

So that was it. That was the link between them. That was the connection that told him there was more to this story than a dead child, a tragedy for a man called Rolfe, and life in an asylum for a crazed woman named Elsie Grant.

I was standing on the opposite corner, he read. *It was snowing hard at the time, and the visibility was poor. I noticed the pram because of its colour; a very bright royal blue. I saw the woman wheel the pram away, but I didn't think there was anything amiss till much later. Yes, I saw her face, and I remember thinking there was an odd look about it. No, I can't really describe what I mean, but it was wolfish somehow, and the hair was drawn down at either side, like a screen. No, I couldn't swear on oath, but I'm almost certain it was the prisoner.*

The name of that witness was John Flack.

Vanin turned another page, but there was nothing more to interest him; just more accounts of Rolfe's career, and a brief story of his wife opening a new hospital wing. Nothing made sense to him, nothing seemed to fit together, but he had at least established a connection between Flack and Rolfe. Flack had been a witness at that trial and, years later, he had seen a picture of someone or something he called the Gaunt Woman. He looked back at the press photograph of Elsie Grant, "gaunt" was right. "Gaunt" was the only word to describe the bent, angular body straining away from the jeering crowd of women round the police cordon. As he looked at the picture, a little germ of an idea started to grow in Vanin's head. It was just a small idea, but very horrible—far, far worse than anything he had imagined possible. All the same, it was all he had to go on, and he would follow it through.

But he had to leave now. He had hoped to find much more

than a book of press cuttings, but there was no time to look longer. Flack might have built his room like a military bunker, with concrete walls and floor, but already the fire was out of control. He dashed for the passage, feeling heat wrap around him like a blanket, and seeing a great orange wave flow over Flack's body. He twisted past it and just managed to reach the front door.

He was on his way at last, and he had something to go on, and a lot of people to see. They included a policeman who had retired, a woman who had been locked away, and a rich man who was afraid. There was also another person he hadn't bargained for.

"Now let's see just what we do know." General Kirk leaned back in his chair, smiling at Trubenoff. The papers on his desk were littered as though a bear had rummaged through them, and his ashtray was piled high with cigar stubs.

"And the answer is that we know very little, I'm afraid," Kirk continued. "A few months ago you became interested in the activities of one Kate Reilly. Miss Reilly is an unsuccessful landscape artist who had been a Communist Party member since the age of eighteen. About three years back Miss Reilly seemed to acquire a sudden and undeserved affluence—bought a cottage in Eire, a new flat in St. John's Wood, and a three-thousand-pound Lancia motor car. That was extremely foolish of her. If she'd been satisfied with a Morris or a Ford, you'd probably have spotted nothing amiss.

"However, you do become suspicious, and a fortnight ago the Special Branch bring her in for questioning. Miss Reilly is not the stuff of martyrs and, after a few threats and the promise of immunity, she talks. She talks in great detail, and it seems that she has been a very bad little girl indeed. 'Giving succour to potential enemies of the Crown' are the exact terms I seem to remember. To be precise, she has been meeting agents from behind the imagined curtain at a rendezvous in County Cork and providing them with a front during their stay here. Yes, a very naughty little girl." Kirk clicked his tongue and shook his head sadly.

"However, with your customary verve, Igor, you decide to make use of Miss Reilly. She has been in the habit of receiving her instructions from Gregor Tanek by telephone, which makes her fairly anonymous. You therefore substitute for her another young lady, our own Miss Kate Martin here, and sit back to await results. In due course you get them. A message arrives via Tanek, and Miss Martin goes off to Mizzen Point armed with a particularly blasphemous password." He broke off and frowned slightly at the girl beside Trubenoff.

"By the way, my dear," he said, "I'm sorry about what happened this morning. I'm afraid that sometimes unpleasant things do take place in our job, and we must just accept them."

"It's all right, sir. I'll get over it." Kate started a little at Kirk's comment. The words were almost the same as Peter Vanin had used on the telephone. As she thought about it, she seemed to see a world of suspicion which was not controlled by countries or governments but rather by departments which were always at war. She had heard a little about Colonel Malendin, and she imagined he might be a man very much like Kirk.

"Good, I'm sure you will." Kirk bent over the notes in front of him. "Now, just let's see what they're after. Kate meets this chap Vanin according to schedule, and travels with him to London. She has checked that he is staying at a small hotel in Kensington, but he has told her nothing about his business over here. He did, however, send a letter to an accommodation address in Hammersmith and ask her to see who called for it. The letter appears to have been treated with some stain, probably fuchsin powder, and was collected by a man named John Flack who seems to be a most unpleasant criminal lunatic. By the way, Igor, you're checking on this Flack, I presume?"

"Yes, sir, the local police should be doing that now. But the point is, what should I do about Vanin? Apart from what Kate has told us I haven't any idea of what he's up to. Should I have him followed?"

"No, I don't think so, Igor. Not yet, at any rate. Remember that this Mr. Vanin is a professional—quite an important man in their Department 5. The chances are that he'd spot a tail as easily as you or I would, old man. No, we'll just have to wait and hope that he'll confide in this little lady before too long." He smiled at Kate as he spoke.

"By the way, my dear," Kirk asked, "what's he like? Personally, I mean. A tough citizen?"

"No, not at all, sir." Kate frowned slightly, thinking of Vanin and how he had seemed to crumple up when she mentioned his wife, and how he had looked walking away at the air terminal.

"He's rather a pathetic little man, doing a routine job merely because he's ordered to, I think. He also seems worried about his family in Russia. He looks—well, just like anybody else. He might be a senior clerk, a schoolmaster, a government official—not a very important one."

"Yes, he would do, if he were any good. The good ones always look quite anonymous." Kirk reached into his drawer and pulled out a small black object resembling a button.

"All the same, I'd better have a picture of him for the record, or in case we want to pull him in in a hurry. You know how to use one of these things, I suppose."

"Yes, I know how to use it." Kate took the tiny camera and slipped it into her bag.

"Good. Then let's have a photograph next time you meet him. I always like to have our files up to date. And did I notice a slight mixture of condescension in your voice just now when you described him as a rather pathetic little man? If so, you can cut it out right away. You've done very well so far, but one false move and Mr. Vanin will be on to you. Whatever happens, don't underrate him." Kirk paused for a moment, staring at the dossier before him, his mutilated hand drumming quietly on the desk.

"Just listen to this pathetic little man's record, will you?" he went on. "At the age of sixteen Peter Vanin was enrolled at the Secret Police Academy at Leningrad. This was probably the most important step in his life. Only the élite go there, and Colonel General Serov was one of its most distinguished products.

"After his training Vanin was sent to Germany for two years attached to the Russian foreign intelligence branch, and by all accounts he did some very important work on armament figures and so on. When Russia was attacked he went home and in '43 came to England ostensibly as a minor official at their embassy. I'd be very interested to know what information he got from us at that time.

"When the war finished we find him in Poland searching out what were described as Undesirable Political Elements; you can guess what that means. The last we hear of him is in Bucharest. There he held the position of Soviet adviser to the Rumanian Secret Police." Kirk closed the folder and pushed it away from him. "Yes, quite a bright boy, this pathetic little man. See you don't underrate him, my dear."

"I won't, sir." Kate looked at Kirk's face and then turned away. On the surface it was like the face of a bluff country squire, but only on the surface. She knew it was capable of kindness and affection, but not of mercy. Mercy had no part in Kirk's make-up. He would order the death of an enemy in much the same way as a squire would tell his gamekeeper to put down vermin.

"No, I won't underrate Vanin," she said, and then broke off, and only thought the rest of the sentence. *I won't underrate him, but I might just get fond of him.*

And, at about the same time that she was speaking, a pleasant Christmas party was drawing to a close. The hostess with forced heartiness had pulled the last cracker and thrust a glass of cheap champagne into the hand of a guest who didn't want it, when she smelled burning, a stale, choking smell of burning, like garlic left too long in a very hot pan.

With curses on all smokers in her heart, she glanced round

the room and across the bright, only-just-paid-for carpet. Then she crossed to the window and pulled back the curtains. As she did so she started to scream.

The house opposite, belonging to a most unpleasant recluse whom the whole neighbourhood disliked, was a mass of flames.

CHAPTER VII

Vanin was waiting for Kate at the Coventry Street "Corner House" as they had arranged on the phone. A morning paper was spread out in front of him, open at the sporting page. He appeared to be reading an account of a football match between Arsenal and Real Madrid with marked interest.

"Ah, there you are." He pushed aside the paper and stood up smiling. It was a warm, friendly smile, but she took care not to look at it too closely, for she remembered her thoughts as Kirk had read the dossier: *I won't underrate him, but I might get fond of him.*

She sat down opposite him, ordered a cup of tea from the waitress, and accepted the cigarette he rather shyly held out to her. As they sat there they resembled any one of a dozen couples in the room. He might have been a middle-aged, misunderstood, and not too successful businessman confiding his troubles to a pretty secretary.

"Now I'm afraid I've got two more jobs for you," he said. "They are jobs which may be—how do you say it? . . . Yes, wild goose chases. You see, they both concern something that happened a long time ago, and the persons concerned may well be dead." He broke off as the waitress fussed round them with Kate's tea, and pulled hard at his cigarette.

"Tell me," he said, when at last the waitress had left them, "does the name Elsie Grant mean anything to you?"

"Elsie Grant? Let me see. It does seem to ring a bell, though it's a very faint one." Kate concentrated hard.

"Yes, of course—she was a murderess, wasn't she? I seem to remember reading about it somewhere. She killed a child. A long time ago—during the war, wasn't it?"

"Yes, that's right. It was in 1940, and she killed not one but three children. She was convicted of murder, but found insane. They put her in an asylum. Well, Kate,"—somehow the name came automatically to him—"I'm not allowed to tell you why, or give you any details, but this woman Grant is of interest to us. I want you to find out where she is. She may be still locked up, she may have been set free, or she may be dead. But if she's alive and still in this country, I want to know where."

"Very well, I'll try." Kate made a note in her pocket book to allow herself time to think. It didn't make sense at all. What possible connection could there be between a Soviet agent and an English murderess who was convicted twenty years ago?

"And the second job?" She leaned forward with the little glass button of her jacket pointing up at his face, her hand toying with the camera switch in her sleeve.

"The second job is similar, and may also be a wild goose chase." The phrase seemed to give him pleasure. "One of those children that Grant killed was the son of Sir Martin Rolfe—you've probably heard of him—the economist."

"Yes, of course I've heard of him." Kate smiled at the question, for who hadn't heard of Martin Rolfe? It was hardly possible to open a paper without seeing a picture of that scholarly face with an account of his activities: committees and enquiries and figures; figures so vast that they seemed incomprehensible to a normal mind. At last she felt she was starting to get somewhere. Kirk would be very curious to hear of Vanin's interest in anything to do with Martin Rolfe—the man who would speak for Britain at the coming conference.

"And so?" She pressed her sleeve and the little camera winked silently. Whatever happened, Kirk would get his picture.

"And so, I want to know about that baby, Kate—all about it. I want you to try and trace the doctor who delivered it, and if he's still alive, you must get him to talk. I can't tell you any more at the moment, as I'm still working in the dark myself. I just want to know everything about that child which Elsie Grant killed."

"Everything?"

"Yes, all you can get. Weight, state of health, colour of eyes, length of mother's pregnancy—everything."

"Very well, I'll do my best, though it's probably going to be difficult. Twenty years ago—a long time." Once again Kate took up her pencil and made a note. The task would have been almost impossible had she been an ordinary person. She wasn't ordinary, though. With Kirk and the help of the department behind her, a lot of doors might be opened. Doors to an insane murderess and a doctor who had delivered a child twenty years ago. It was rather amusing that a Soviet spy should get his information through the co-operation of the British Intelligence Service.

"And is that all?" she asked, smiling slightly.

"Yes, that's all." Vanin finished his coffee, and pushed back the chair. "I'd like to tell you one more thing though, my dear. I'm very pleased that we're working together—very pleased indeed." For a moment his hand rested on her arm. "You know, under different circumstances . . . Yes, I think we could be good for each other." He gave her a final, rather prim smile and folded his paper.

"I'll ring you tomorrow," he said and walked away towards the line of phone booths by the door.

Vanin had two calls to make, and he took the least important first. Almost as the bell rang, that quiet, anonymous, but still foreign voice answered him.

"Homeway," he said. "Homeway Products, 8-5," and a moment later he was giving his instructions to Gregor Tanek. He was glad to give them, for, although he was a Russian, he liked to keep promises. In a few hours, Michael Arabin's family would be on their way to England.

He replaced the phone and started to dial another number—the most famous number in England.

*

Superintendent George Pode, formerly of the Criminal Investigation Department, but since retirement the bane of his wife, the blight of the West Hampstead Golf Club, and the prize bore of the "Feathers" saloon bar, was only too happy to lunch with the press. He said it long and loudly over the phone, and he said it again, standing in the foyer of Kethner's restaurant—*Internationally Known, Service our Speciality*—pumping Vanin's hand up and down.

"Good of you," he boomed, for the whole room to hear. "Very good of you indeed. Always ready to help you chaps out with a story. Yes, of course—a drink or two before we eat would be just the ticket." He swaggered forward, lowered his vast bulk onto a bar stool, and took a cigarette that Vanin offered, beaming as he did so.

"Haven't been in this dump for years, as it happens, though I used it a lot in the old days; before I retired. Seem to remember that Chateaubriand was the speciality then, and they did you proud. . . . Thanks, old chap, a large whiskey would be just what I could use. Make it Haig, barman, and just a touch of water." As if by a conjuring trick, the glass seemed to vanish in his enormous hand, and when he put it down it was empty.

"Ah, that's much better. . . . Yes, I will have a refill, if you don't mind. Makes no difference to you fellows on expense accounts, does it?" He roared with unnecessary laughter and struck Vanin a hard and painful blow over his left kidney.

"What paper did you say you were on, by the way? My memory is getting a bit rusty these days. Ah, yes, the Detroit *Sunday Herald*. Never heard of it, but I dare say it's all it should be. You're not American though, are you? Not by birth, at least. Thought I noticed an accent just now."

"No, I was born in Poland, but I've been an American citizen for ten years."

"I see. That explains it. Had to hook it from those Bolshevik bastards, I suppose. 'Needs must when the devil drives,' eh?" Pode had a heavy, pinkish face, a flowing white moustache, and the most self-satisfied expression that Vanin had ever seen.

"And now, should we talk business? Scotland Yard gave you my phone number, and I understand that you're doing some articles on notable European police officers. Very naturally you want to include me in the series. Well, let's get down to the important thing. I'm not a man to be troubled by false modesty, neither am I a man who expects to work for nothing. 'The labourer is worthy of his hire,' and all that. Just how much will your paper pay?"

"I'm afraid that rather depends on what my editor thinks of the article, Superintendent." Vanin smiled and drew out his book of traveller's checks. "This is just a preliminary interview, of course, and I'll have to show him something in writing before he names a definite figure. At the same time, I was asked to give you three hundred dollars as proof of our good faith—just a retainer, as it were."

"Thanks." Pode took the signed check and grinned—a big, wide grin that lit up his whole face.

"Three hundred, eh? Fair enough for a start—very fair in fact. Just over a hundred quid at the present rate of exchange. A bobby on the beat gets a thousand these days, of course, but all the same this will come in very handy." He stuffed the check away and pulled himself off the stool.

"And now, Mr. Vane—sorry, Vanin, I'm quite at your disposal. Let's eat and have a yarn, shall we? I enjoy talking a great deal and, as you can imagine, I've plenty to tell. After, though I say it myself, an extremely successful career, it's about time somebody put it down in black and white." He began to walk heavily towards the restaurant, and then paused with a sudden frown on his face.

"By the way, who else are you including in these articles of yours? Not Carmichael, I hope—not Inspector Willis?"

"No, neither of them, sir." Vanin noted a trace of bitterness in Pode's voice that told of petty jealousies and rivalries stretching back across the years. "As it happens, you're the only British police officer we're including in the series. My editor felt your story should be good enough to make any others unnecessary."

"And he was dead right too. Credit where credit is due, eh?" Pode's face lit up again with good humour. "Now let's order, shall we?"

He lowered himself into a chair and picked up the huge embossed menu. "Though I say it myself, I understand food." His eyes ran greedily down the card, and then he turned to the head waiter. "Well, my boy, what's nice today?"

"Everything is nice, sir—as always." The man bore a marked resemblance to the late Pope Pius XII, and he winced slightly, looking as though he were sucking a lemon and not liking it.

"Good, I'm glad to hear it. My friend here is from the United States and he's used to the best—the very best, waiter. Just see that he gets it. Now let me think." As Pode made his selection, Vanin noticed that it seemed to be made by price as much as by choice. He obviously intended to make the most of somebody else's expense account. He shook his head sadly as Vanin ordered veal.

"Here, what's that, old boy? You've messed things up, I'm afraid. Can't drink red wine with that and I can't have white with my steak. We'll just have to compromise with a rosé, I'm afraid. Bring us a bottle of the Château d'Eclus '55, waiter, and see that it's properly chilled." He leaned back in his chair in pleasurable anticipation of the meal.

"Funny thing your choosing this place, Mr. Vanin. I had the pleasure of depriving a chap of his liberty in here once. We arrested him at that corner table, I seem to remember. Yes, Jack Thursday it was—one of the best con men in the business, though you wouldn't think it to look at him. Funny little beggar, less than five and a half foot tall. Started from nothing as well, doing the split-pound trick round Manchester."

"The split-pound trick?" Vanin raised his eyebrows in purely professional curiosity.

"Yes, that's right; common enough dodge before the war. You need two chaps for it. One of 'em rather nondescript, the other imposing and obviously the soul of honesty. You and I would fit the bill to a tee.

"Well, you go into a shop and buy a packet of fags—a shilling they were in those days. You pay with a pound note, and get your packet and nineteen shillings change. Out you go.

"About five minutes later I walk in. Buy another packet, and pay with a ten-shilling note. Nine shillings change to come? Oh, dear no. 'Sorry, miss, but that was a pound I gave you. As a matter of fact, I can tell you the number. I always jot them down for safety's sake. Here it is—282673—and if you look in your till I think you'll find it. Thank you.' Humble apologies from the shop girl, and ten shillings' profit a time. Not bad money in the thirties."

"No, I suppose not." Vanin remembered the trick well. For some unknown reason it was known as a Nicholai Ruble in Moscow.

"Ah, here we are." Pode beamed at the approaching waiters and tucked the napkin into his collar, preparing to enjoy himself.

But between courses he talked—how he talked. After the soup, he discussed the breaking up of a gang of forgers, a most brilliant piece of work in every way. Before the steak, he told of a murderer brought to book by painstaking attention to detail. Between the *marrons glacés* and the cheese, of a scandal—hushed up by tact and self-sacrifice—regarding the sexual habits of a middle-aged statesman. All the triumphs of law and order brought about by the intelligence, cleverness, bravery, and devotion of that scourge of crime, Superintendent George Pode.

"St. George," as he assured Vanin his colleagues had called him. "St. George will have the blighter under lock and key—Put good old George on the case and things will start to hum—Nah, the super don't let no grass grow under his boots." Only at the end of the enormous meal did Pode ease back his chair, sniff the brandy suspiciously as though it were not quite what he was accustomed to, and address Vanin directly.

"Well, that was very nice, old chap, very nice indeed. Makes me wish I was born hollow. Can't think when I've eaten so well, though I'm sure you've enjoyed yourself too—got a good deal of material to go on. By the way, what's your Christian name? I never could stand on ceremony. . . .

"Peter, eh? Well, Pete, let's get to work. Just what kind of article had you in mind? Do you want a general account of my career, or should we concentrate on one particular case?"

"One case would be best, I think." Vanin motioned towards the waiter as he answered. Another brandy or so and Pode would be ready to talk—to talk as Vanin wanted him to.

"Fair enough. Though it will be difficult to select the most interesting out of so many. What about Mason and Reade, those Brighton forgers I was telling you about, or the Croydon bank job?"

"No, I don't think so. You see, we're a Sunday paper, and our readers want something a little sordid for their morning's entertainment. The editor felt that the case of Elsie Grant might fit the bill."

"Elsie Grant!" A curious expression suddenly flitted across Pode's face as he repeated the name—a slightly guilty expression, but not very guilty. The look of a child detected in some minor naughtiness.

"Oh, no, I doubt if that would do. It was all rather dull, really—just unpleasant, as these nut cases always are. If you want something sordid, what about old Dr. Rankin? He was a lad, if ever there was. Cut up his wife and housemaid and dumped them into the main sewer at Weybridge. That's a good yarn if you like, and though I say it myself, the investigation was conducted most brilliantly—threw a lot of credit on all concerned.

"Yes, 1946 it was. Rankin had been having an affair with the maid for—" He started to launch into the story, but Vanin cut him short.

"No, I'm sorry, Superintendent," he said. "It really is the Grant case we're interested in—only the Grant case."

"Very well, if I must, I must; though I think you're making a mistake." Pode took another swig at his brandy, and blew his nose with quite unnecessary violence.

"A sad little case that, concerning a very sad person. Elsie Grant was one of those people who seem doomed from the start; almost as though the cards were stacked against them at birth. Orphanage child she was, and very plain—one shoulder higher than the other—employed as a maid of all work in a slum boardinghouse—no bed of roses in those days. Cinderella, in fact, waiting for the fairy godmother."

"And did she turn up, this fairy godmother?"

"Yes, she turned up all right—*he* did, rather. His name was Littlewood—the gentleman who runs the football pools. Elsie put her row of noughts and crosses in the correct squares and, in due course, a check arrived. Over a thousand quid it was, but I can't remember the exact amount. Anyway, a nice sum of money by pre-war values.

"Well, Cinderella had her glass slippers now, and in due course Prince Charming came on the scene; that bastard Leonard Grant. They were married in church—she wasn't to know he had a wife already—and after the proper interval a child arrived. Two days later Grant hooked it, taking all her money except twenty pounds. He did at least have the decency to leave that."

"And the baby died, didn't it?"

"No, it didn't die, Pete. It was killed. Murdered, if I had a hand in making the laws of England. Elsie goes round to the labour exchange looking for a job, and leaves the pram on the pavement. While she's inside, along comes a drunk in a sports car, takes a corner too fast, mounts the curb, and bang! Down comes baby and cradle and all." As though to emphasize the point, Pode's hand came crashing down on the table, to the consternation of their fellow diners. From his vantage point by the door, Mr. Kethner himself, a resplendent figure in silk-lined tails, seemed on the verge of apoplexy.

"Yes," continued Pode, oblivious, "I remember the driver got two years for manslaughter, but that didn't do Elsie any good."

"She went insane?"

"That's right, Pete. She went crazy—right round the bend. A hospital took her in as a voluntary patient for a time, but she came out ten days before Christmas. Two days later we got the first killing.

"Well, we couldn't get much sense out of her during our examination, nor could the doctors. Today she'd have been put down as unfit to plead, but that wasn't common then. From what we could make out, her mind had refused to accept the accident, and she was looking for her own child. She'd see an unattended pram and wheel it home, a rented house in Fulham. The children had all died through suffocation. Probably she cuddled them a little too tightly.

"And that's about all there was to it, I'm afraid. Just a nasty, sad little story, and quite uninteresting. We were tipped off by a suspicious neighbour. God bless all suspicious people, by the way." Pode raised his glass in a mock toast.

"No, there was no real police work at all. We just got a warrant and searched the house. The two bodies were hidden under the stairs. Why your editor should be interested in the case I can't imagine."

"Just a moment, Superintendent." There was a sudden eager gleam in Vanin's eye. "What did you say just then?"

"What did I say, Pete? Said I thought your editor was barmy to wish to dig it up, when there's so much better material to hand. Now the Royston murders, for instance; yes, I'd just been promoted Inspector, I remember, and—"

"No, I'm sorry, Mr. Pode, but I'm not interested in the Royston case; just the case of Elsie Grant. You said two bodies just now, though the papers reported there were three." He pulled out his notebook.

"Yes, here we are. *James Harbin, aged six weeks—Pamela Thurston, seven—the Rolfe child, one month old and not yet christened.* Just why did you say you found only two bodies, Superintendent?"

"Why, it's—it's a long time ago, isn't it, Pete? Perhaps my memory is getting rusty. As I said, the case never interested me very much." Once again that slightly guilty expression crept across Pode's face.

"All right, let's have the truth, shall we?" Vanin leaned forward across the table. "My editor will pay well for your story, but only for the full story. Just what did you really find?"

"All right, I'll tell you. I was covering up a little—in a way, that is. It can't do any harm now, and my pension is secure enough. Yes, I held something back from the press, but if you were a cop you'd understand why." Pode's smug, rather asinine expression seemed to alter, and he looked what he had been: a tough, efficient policeman who lived for the job.

"Nut cases are always the worst things we have to deal with, for two reasons. Firstly, there is never an obvious connection between the killer and the victim, as in the case of murder for gain, for example. Secondly—"

"Secondly, they attract imitators." Vanin's words came out automatically, as he remembered his own police training.

"Quite right, Pete. They attract imitation. One loony kills a girl, say, in a certain manner and in a certain place—a churchyard, for example. Well, having read the glowing reports you chaps write about it, another nut is tempted to follow his example and strike a similar blow for freedom. And if that happens, and the news gets out, then the whole thing is liable to snowball." There was a great bitterness in Pode's voice. "And I didn't want that to happen in the Grant case. I didn't want it at all, because I'm very fond of kids."

"You mean—"

"I mean, Pete, that, on my own responsibility, a slightly contrived version of the facts was given to the press. I didn't want any more children killed, and I didn't want anyone to follow Elsie Grant's example. Also I didn't want it rumoured that anybody already had."

"Go on, Superintendent. So, you did conceal something?"

"Yes, I concealed something all right. Oh, don't worry—Elsie Grant was guilty. She pleaded guilty to the first murder, of James Harbin, and was sentenced on that charge. If she hadn't, everything would have had to come out in court automatically. No, there was never any doubt about it. We found those kids under the stairs."

"You found *two* of them." Clickety—clickety—click! Like a metal puzzle, the pieces in Vanin's head were starting to fit together.

"But what about the third? Were you quite certain she killed that third child—the Rolfe baby?"

"The third?" Pode belched slightly, and his eyes were puffy with too much food and alcohol.

"Oh, yes, we were certain all right—quite certain. I talked to Elsie Grant for hours, and I'm sure she killed the three of them. She was guilty all right, as guilty as hell. All the same, in the case of the Rolfe child there was one rather peculiar feature. . . .

"Yes, that's right, Pete. We never found the body."

CHAPTER VIII

Kate's first job had been easy, for Elsie Grant was dead. She had died a long time ago, during the war. It only took a telephone call to find that out.

A Dornier bomber, beaten back from London by fog and the barrage, had turned for home with its cargo intact. Twenty miles from the Kent coast, the fog had thinned slightly and, almost overhead, the pilot had made out the silhouette of a Spitfire. He had dived automatically and as he did so a group of red brick buildings had loomed up before him. With speed and the loss of weight his only object, the solution had been obvious. The observer's hand had tightened on a switch, and the land mine they carried went swinging down through the mist. It fell on the women's wing of Broadhurst Asylum, and twenty-three sick minds were able to sleep at last.

Her second job hadn't been so easy, however. It had taken the department a full hour even to find the name of the doctor who had attended Lady Rolfe, and when they knew it they seemed no further forward. The man seemed completely elusive; he had maintained a general practice in Kensington till three years ago, and then nothing—nothing at all. It appeared that he had just sold up and gone away. The National Health files could tell them little, and even the Inland Revenue Office didn't know where he was. There was just one address that might give them a lead: his mother-in-law's, a restaurant in a mid-Sussex town.

It was a lovely day, though. Probably the last fine day of the year, and Kate drove slowly through bright winter sunlight, with the snow still fresh and clean on the hills. There was no need to hurry. Vanin would not be contacting her before tomorrow morning, and she wanted to think. It seemed as if she was getting somewhere at last; or at least Kirk appeared to think so. As she told him of Vanin's instructions, there had been a sudden flash of interest in his eyes, and the heavy, cynical face had looked almost boyish—young, and eager, and full of excitement. The look of a terrier who doesn't know exactly where the rat is hiding, but feels that it must be very near.

"So, that's it, is it? Our friend is taking an interest in Martin Rolfe, is he? In something that happened to Martin Rolfe a long time ago. And I wonder why. All very strange, isn't it? Rolfe is an important man, but what possible interest can that murder have to a Soviet agent? 'Curiouser and curiouser,' said Alice.

"I've met Rolfe once or twice, as it happens," Kirk went on. "Don't know him well, of course—not at all my kind of chap, but we use the same club, and I can tell you one thing, my dear. If Rolfe has a skeleton in his cupboard, it will be a very nasty one indeed. He's a proud man, you see, but only on the surface. Underneath I think he feels desperately insecure, and needs power and popular esteem as an alcoholic needs a drink. A very dangerous man, if someone threatened to take that esteem away from him....

"Well, you're doing very nicely now, little lady, and we'll

just have to help Mr. Vanin to find out what he wants to know. And when he's done that, when we know what he wants with Rolfe, then I'll be right behind him. Yes, I feel I'm going to enjoy this case." Kirk turned away, concluding the interview, and once again Kate noticed the sudden cold expression that came over his face.

But though she drove slowly, every journey has its end, and she had reached hers now. She turned up the steep, winding hill into Saxonfield High Street, and parked the car. Before she got out she checked the equipment that Kirk had given her: a press card and an envelope that felt fat and comfortable round its cache of five-pound notes.

The "Olde Copper Kettle" restaurant stood on a corner, and there was no mistaking it. The battered utensil that provided its name swayed from a wrought-iron frame, and a sign in heavy Gothic type swung below it. It was just like any of the thousand immensely genteel, completely sham and ridiculous establishments that dot the southern half of England.

Kate pushed open the bead-draped door, lowering her head beneath a worm-eaten beam, and groped her way forward through the semi-darkness. The tables were low and tiled, there were reproduction Speed maps on the walls, and shapeless and inflammable objects woven from straw hung from the mock-Tudor ceiling. The beams on the ceiling looked as though they concealed some pretty substantial girders to hold them in position. Over the fireplace hung a pokerwork motto. As her eyes grew accustomed to the light, she was able to read what it said:

Rest awhile, traveller, and take your fill here
Of Comfort and Kindness, and good Sussex Cheer.

"Kindness" might be in order, but she felt that "Comfort" was a barefaced lie. Her knees were pressed hard against the sharp edge of the table, and the "Sussex Cheer" seemed a long time in materializing. She waited a good five minutes for service while, in the corner, two grim females in masculine tweed coats eyed her critically, and then fell to discussing the wicked ways of a high-church clergyman.

"*Father* indeed! Parading himself in the street in a cloak and flicking holy water in the aisle. Filling the church up with painted images, and making the choir learn that new-fangled Plainsong nonsense. A bit too plain for my taste, it is, and I told him so to his face. He didn't seem to care at all, though I've been on the Ladies' Committee for twelve years. What old Canon Rusper would have said I can't imagine. Enough to make the poor dear turn in his grave—"

There was a little brass bell on the table, and when the five minutes were up Kate lifted it and rang it nervously.

"Did you want something?" The waitress had appeared out of a door in the shadows, a powder compact still in her hand. She was young and pretty, but her face was sullen. The face of an employee who is doubtful when the next wages will be coming. Kate ordered tea and scones as humbly as she could, and only when they were pushed in front of her did she bring out her question.

"Does a Dr. Fenwick live here?"

"*Doctor* Fenwick? No, there's no doctor here, miss. Only Mrs. Fenwick and her Mum." The girl frowned slightly. "I believe she had a husband once, but I dunno what happened to him. Went away, I think, and I can't say I blame him." She leaned forward conversationally.

"I 'aven't been 'ere long meself, and between you and me, I don't intend to stay long either. Goin' to fold, this place is, and I don't intend to fold with it. No, this rat's not going down with any sinking ship—not on your Nellie. Ta, miss." She took the half crown that Kate held out. "I'll get Ma Fenwick for you."

The woman who came into the room a minute later was made for persecution. She had a mild, sheeplike face, she wore bangles, and her grey hair was tied back with a faded blue ribbon. She looked as though her only business, her one purpose in life, had been the taking of orders. Orders from employers, from bullying husbands, from aged and demanding relatives—any orders, so long as they were firmly given. She bowed humbly to the two grim females in the corner and then hurried towards Kate with a nervous smile on her lips. A string of green beads round her neck made a sharp clicking noise.

"Good afternoon, madam. Bessie said you wanted to speak to me. I do hope you've nothing to complain of." The low, gentle voice sounded as though it were very used to complaints.

"No, of course not. Everything is very nice. It's purely about a personal matter that I wanted to talk to you. You are the wife of Dr. Robert Fenwick, I believe?"

"Yes, yes, I'm his wife, Miss—thank you—Miss Reilly. I was his wife that is, till—" The eyes suddenly looked as though they were about to fill with tears.

"Oh, I'm so sorry, Mrs. Fenwick. I didn't know that your husband was dead."

"Dead? Oh, no, he's not dead. At least I don't think so. It's just that we—that he—" She broke off, looking behind her towards the two prying faces at the corner table.

"Would you care to come upstairs to my flat, Miss Reilly? It's quiet there, and we could talk. That is if you don't mind—but if you have news of Bob—" She helped Kate to move back her chair and led the way to a staircase that lay behind the door.

The room above the café was small and chintzy and bright, but completely cheerless. Though the weather was icy, the single bar of a small electric fire was its only heating, and the chair covers had a dead, faded look that came from too much washing. Only one wall looked rich and prosperous. A bookcase stood against it, filled with bright bindings, and Kate could read the titles on their spines: *Hood and Polinger's Surgery, Benham's Standard Midwifery, Hill and Jackson's Physiology.* To the right of the bookcase there was an opening into another room, screened by a curtain. From time to time, Kate heard a creak of boards and heavy, slow movements from behind it.

"Now, Miss Reilly, what did you want to talk to me about?" The woman fussed round her as Kate sat down. "Have you any news about my husband? You see, he left me some time ago, but I wondered if perhaps he'd been trying to get in touch with me. A very wicked woman made him leave me, and she might have stopped him writing—"

"I'm afraid I haven't any news." Kate glanced at a photograph of Dr. Fenwick on the mantelpiece. The man's face was handsome, but strangely without character. It had good eyes, a pleasing nose and mouth, and a firm chin, but somehow they didn't seem to match, to fit together to give a personality. All the same, it didn't look the kind of face which could be *made* to do anything.

"No, it's information from you that I want," said Kate. "Do you have your husband's address, Mrs. Fenwick? Is he in England?"

"Oh, no, he's not in England. He went abroad with her. The last I heard was that they were in Jamaica."

"I see. Then I'd better explain the position to you, Mrs. Fenwick. I've not really come about your husband so much as about a case he worked on a long time ago. You see, I'm a journalist and—" Kate pulled out her press card, and began to tell the prepared story just as Vanin, with Kirk's approval, had told her to tell it. She was a good, fluent liar, and it came easily: she was writing a series on crimes of the past, and because of Rolfe's present important position the murder of his child was to be included. She told it well and, when she had finished, Mrs. Fenwick sat down beside her, obviously convinced.

"Yes, I see. As it happens, I remember the case quite well. I was sorry for the little boy, of course, but this Rolfe must have been a horrible man. Poor Bob was so upset at the time."

"Horrible!" Kate raised her eyebrows slightly. "Just why do you say that?"

"Well, he was so rude for one thing. A few days after the child was born, Bob went round to see him about something. I've no idea what it was. Bob never talked shop to me, but I know he was worried. Anyway Rolfe behaved most disgracefully. He became violent and abusive and ordered Bob to leave his house. I remember feeling when the baby was killed it might have been some kind of judgment on him. . . . Oh dear! That was a terrible thing to say. I'm so sorry, and I didn't mean it, of course. It's just that my husband was always such a kind, gentle man. It seemed so wrong—so unfair on Rolfe's part."

"It's all right; I can understand how you must have felt, Mrs. Fenwick." Kate considered her next move, and her eyes fell on the bookcase. "But I see that you still have your husband's textbooks," she said. "Have you perhaps his papers too? Any documents relating to that Rolfe baby?"

"His papers? Yes, I think I have them. When Bob went away, he left everything behind—except money and the clothes he was wearing. His notebooks should be in the tin trunk in the bedroom. Bob was so methodical, you know. He made notes on every case that interested him. The Rolfe baby must be there." Her face broke into a sudden look of mistrust. "But, Miss Reilly, you don't mean—"

"Yes, I mean that I want to look at those notebooks, Mrs. Fenwick. My agency will pay well too. A hundred pounds—in cash—now." She started to open her bag as she spoke.

"No, no, no! I really couldn't allow that. Whatever you paid me, I couldn't allow it." Mrs. Fenwick's crushed, humble face took on a certain dignity in anger. "You just don't understand, do you? A doctor's reports on his patients are sacred, like what a priest hears in the confessional. And my husband was a good doctor too—a good man. He was just tired at the end, that was all. The extra paper work from that wretched National Health Scheme tired him. He had to have a change, and then that wretched woman—" She got up and pulled open the door: a servant showing out the unwelcome guest at her master's orders. "Yes, I'm afraid I want you to leave now, Miss Reilly. My husband was a good man, and I still treasure his memory, whatever he may have done."

"Your husband, my dear Lucy, was and is a bastard." The

voice came from behind them, and Kate swung round on her heel, looking at the curtained doorway by the bookcase.

The curtains were drawn back now, and a woman stood framed between them: a big, heavy woman, dressed in black and leaning on a stick. By her features, it was possible to guess that she was Mrs. Fenwick's mother, but there was only a physical resemblance between them. This woman had never taken an order in her life.

"Now just sit down, Lucy, and listen to me. That goes for you as well, Miss Reilly. I've been listening to what you said, and you interested me." She watched them settle themselves in front of her like guilty children before she went on.

"Thank you. Now, Miss Reilly, I'm going to tell you something. My son-in-law Robert Fenwick was what my generation used to call a *bounder.* He merely married my daughter because she had a little money of her own and he wanted to buy a fashionable practice. Don't interrupt me, Lucy!" Her stick came down with a crash on the floor.

"But, when someone younger, and richer, and more *entertaining* came his way,"—there was a marked pronunciation of the word—"Dr. Fenwick decided to break loose. He sold his practice, because he dreaded scandal, and persuaded us to move down here. Once we had the café going, he cut and ran. At the moment, I imagine he is lying on some beach with his mistress—the half-caste daughter of a West Indian banana millionaire. One of his late patients, I may say.

"Now, Miss Reilly, let's talk business. You want to have a look at Robert Fenwick's papers, and they are in my possession." She pivoted slightly on her stick as she spoke. "Well, you mentioned a hundred pounds just now, and it's not enough. Could you manage two hundred, do you think?"

"Yes, I can pay two hundred." Kate opened her bag and pulled out the envelope. Two hundred was the exact sum they had given her and there was no time to bargain.

"Thank you." The woman took the notes from her and started to count them carefully.

"No, Lucy," she said. "Please don't try to argue with me. I'm very sorry, but this is how I want it. In fact, Miss Reilly is like a fairy godmother, and we should be very glad of her sudden interest in Bob's career. As you know, we owe money to the landlord, to the electricity company, and to the council for rates. We owe Cook and Bessie two weeks' wages. We owe far too much money to everybody. Miss Reilly's contribution may just carry us through till the summer, when we hope to do more business. As far as we are concerned, your husband is dead. I, however, intend to go on living. Yes, quite correct, Miss Reilly; two hundred pounds." She tucked the notes back into their envelope. "Now, will you wait here a moment, please."

The old lady walked through the curtains and a minute later came back with a battered tin box, which she laid on the table.

"Here you are, my dear. This is what you asked for. All the good doctor's reports, written down in his own fair hand. I hope you will find what you need." She opened the lid, and took her daughter by the arm.

"Come, Lucy," she said. "Miss Reilly has kept her side of the bargain, so let's keep ours. Let her examine her treasure trove in peace."

Fair hand was a good description. Whatever his faults, Robert Fenwick had kept his notes neatly and legibly. Kate laid the notebooks and clipped papers on the table and bent over them. The last book was dated just over three years ago, the first in 1933. On the mantlepiece at her side, a little clock ticked above the picture of their author, and his notes ticked with them. Nineteen thirty-four—thirty-seven—forty; January, April, November. And, at last, there it was. Almost in the centre of a page was the entry she wanted.

November 23rd. Rolfe, 32, Lawrence Gdns—Today I delivered a Man *child.* There was a line drawn under the word *Man,* but nothing else. No record of weight, condition, or length of mother's pregnancy—nothing to help her at all.

Kate turned a page. The next entry concerned a woman

with a diseased hipbone, and the three that followed were equally irrelevant. And then, she had the thread again.

Rolfe, Lawrence Gdns. Matthews gave me the result of the biological tests today, and I'm afraid there is no doubt about it. Yes, the thousand to one chance I dreaded has come off. If there is a God, then I think he may have forsaken some of us. Below the sentences there were four words in Latin.

Very carefully Kate copied down those four words, and then crossed to the bookcase and pulled out the necessary volumes of Palin's Dictionary. She had studied Latin at school, and she had been trained as a nurse. Already she had a slight idea of what they might mean. She didn't like it at all.

As she thumbed through the books, she suddenly felt cold and alone in the chintzy little room. Behind the curtain she could hear low murmurs from Mrs. Fenwick and her mother, but they weren't like voices at all so much as automatic sounds: waves lapping on a cold, deserted shore at the very edge of the world.

Kate turned up her coat collar and lit a cigarette. Then she began to read the final line of print that could make certainty of her suspicion. There was suddenly a great pain behind her eyes as she did so. Dr. Fenwick had been right, it seemed. The chances were about a thousand to one. Two uncommon complaints had joined forces in one human child, and the sum they added up to was terror.

If it had lived, the Rolfe baby would have become a monster.

CHAPTER IX

"And you're sure, my dear? You checked your facts thoroughly and you're quite, quite certain?" Peter Vanin leaned over the parapet of the Serpentine bridge, half looking at the water and half at Kate.

"It seems almost impossible. A nightmare come to life."

"Yes, it's a nightmare all right, but still true. I checked very carefully, and I do have a little medical training." She reached in her bag and handed him a sheet of paper.

"This is the exact wording I copied from Fenwick's notes, and here is a translation in simple terms. That child was born with *Morbus Crassi,* a disease which was said to affect a certain Roman family. It's a weakness of a group of nerve centres in the brain's frontal lobe. In time they would begin to shrink and lead to lunacy—very violent lunacy, if left untreated."

"And you say it couldn't be treated because of this other illness?"

"Yes, that's right. The child was also born with Deladier's disease. That's a condition of overactivity in the pituitary gland. The secretions would tend to cause bodily deformity, and possibly giantism.

"And the point is that though both those conditions can be treated, and possibly cured nowadays, together you can't touch them. Interfere with the pituitary and that brain condition would spread unchecked and probably kill the patient in weeks. Yes, Fenwick was right when he said that the chances were about a thousand to one. Two rare ailments joining forces, and together they become a nightmare."

"I see. Poor kid—poor—poor little child." Vanin stared down at the ducks floating below him like green-and-brown bottles: fat, over-fed ducks that had gone decadent. They didn't even bother to migrate any more in the midst of London's plenty. All the same, he suddenly wished he had some bread to give them. He would have liked to do that. At the moment he would have liked to do any commonplace family thing.

"So, if it had lived, the Rolfe baby would have been a monster?"

"That's right, Peter. And it was a mercy really, wasn't it?—a mercy that Elsie Grant did kill it."

"Yes, I suppose you could call it that," he said, knowing that he lied, that he didn't think of it as a mercy or a blessing at all. From the point of view of the department it was just a fulcrum and a lever, a way to bring pressure on a certain economist and make him give the wrong answers at the coming conference, a way to break the Anglo-American alliance once and for all.

"And now I think we'd better part company, my dear. You've got what I wanted and you've done very well—very well indeed. I'll see that Gregor Tanek hears about it. . . .

"No, I'm afraid that we probably won't meet again—not unless something goes wrong. I've got two more little jobs to do, and then I'll hand over to someone else and can go home. They said they'd fly me out with some of the embassy personnel—diplomatic immunity, you know." He grinned and took her hand, feeling it very soft and warm in his. Somehow its touch made him feel less alone. "Yes, it's goodbye, my dear, and I don't expect we'll meet again. But thank you—thank you for all the help you've given me." He watched her walk away and then he leaned over the bridge again and considered his next move.

For he had a theory at last—only a theory, a hunch, an idea, but he had to follow it. Even though he were completely wrong and it was as absurd as it sounded, he had to follow it, for it was the only one he had to go on.

Take a very proud couple, he thought—and both the Rolfes were proud . . . He had spent two hours with one of Tanek's very reliable sources of information, and he knew a lot more about Rolfe and his wife now. She had been a Ravensburn before she married him: one of the oldest families in England. Old, proud blood which might carry a little bad seed with it.

And that couple would have been prouder still when they knew a child was on the way. An heir to Rolfe's intelligence and wealth—the direct descendant of a knight who had led a charge at Hastings. Then one day a doctor named Fenwick had walked into their house and shown them exactly what that child would become. Yes, pride would have melted like snow at his words, and Death would have seemed very attractive to that no longer proud couple.

Indeed, Death had already given its examples. Two children

stolen and probably murdered in the neighbourhood—why not a third? If the cards were carefully played no one would suffer, and there would be no shame or disgrace for a man who craved public esteem and a woman whose pride couldn't bear the thought that she had mothered an imbecile.

Yes, those children that Elsie Grant had stolen must have seemed to the couple like a pointer—a lead which Rolfe's keen, mathematical brain could easily have turned to action. Certain instructions to a nursemaid would have been the first move: "On your way back from the Park, Doris, or Mary, or Jane, I want you to stop at the store and buy me this or that. Yes, leave the pram outside. It will be quite safe for a minute or two."

And then, while the maid was inside, another woman had come down the street and wheeled it away. A woman who had every right to do so, for she was the child's mother. The rest was easy to follow. Soft, gentle fingers lowering a pillow towards a face which disease would soon ravage—a little body that didn't take much earth to cover it and, at last, peace. Yes, "Rest in peace, my son."

But he hadn't rested, and there was no peace. Vanin remembered Arabin's description of Lady Rolfe. A tall, over-painted woman shut away in her gloomy, neglected house and dressed like a girl to remind her of the days when she was still young—when her husband didn't draw away from her for fear of another conception—of the time before she became a murderess—of the years when Rolfe spent some of his time with her and wasn't completely drugged by the need for power and approbation.

And then, one day, there wasn't even the delusion of peace, and fear became a companion. A witness at the Grant trial had looked at a certain picture of Lady Rolfe, and the penny had dropped. To John Flack with his hatred of success, it must have seemed like a gift from heaven as he had stared at that picture and remembered a face he had seen through the snow, so many years ago. A trick of light, of angle, of hair styling might have done it—anything might—but it had shown him the truth, and he could get down to his very nasty work: little matchstick drawings with meaningless writing below them—*the Gaunt Woman who can blast you.*

"No!" Vanin suddenly shook his head and spoke aloud. It was preposterous, of course. It couldn't have been like that; there were a hundred reasons against it. He hadn't a single piece of definite evidence to support his case. All the same, as he leaned over that bridge, he suddenly knew that since it was the only theory he had he must play it to the end—the very bitter end. He would beard Rolfe with his preposterous theory, and just hope that he had stumbled on some of the truth. Then, if Rolfe broke, he could hand him over to an economist to be provided by Tanek, and go home.

But if Rolfe didn't break, then he would have failed—and the department didn't recognize failure. His final talk in Malendin's office suddenly came back to him.

"Goodbye, my dear Peter, and good luck," Malendin had said. "And remember something, will you—remember that we are all expendable—that not one of us matters as an individual. Only the M.V.D. and the department matters—only the Party matters, in fact." Malendin had grinned suddenly and raised his hand in a clenched-fist salute, as though addressing a political rally. "Yes, Comrade Vanin, the mills of our Revolution grind well," he had said loudly, and then lowered his voice.

"Pretentious nonsense, of course, Peter, but the idea is true. We are not individuals, but just part of the machine. Whatever the risk, I want you to get this Martin Rolfe. I want you to get him good."

Malendin was a cynical careerist on the surface, but he at least told his subordinates the truth. He, Peter Vanin, had to take every risk in the book, and there was no coming back with a tale of failure. If Rolfe didn't break, then—the little capsule against his teeth suddenly seemed to move, as though with a life of its own.

But it was time to go now. In the distance a clock started

to strike the hour and he adjusted his watch, smiling slightly as he did so. The meeting with Rolfe was not till the evening, and there was another job to do first. This time it was a job he hoped to enjoy.

"Yes, Minister. No, Minister. Yes, I quite understand, Minister." Kirk bent over the intercom on his desk, and his face bore an expression of cynicism, boredom, and rank ill temper. He might have been talking to a dim-witted child.

"Yes, that's quite correct, Minister, and there's nothing to worry about. Yes, we know all about that house in Silver Pine Grove, and the fire last night, and everything is under control. That's right, one of the bodies belonged to the tenant, a man named John Flack, and we're working on the other now. The fire was probably started by a Soviet agent who landed in Eire last Monday. . . . I beg your pardon, Minister." A dark, angry flush spread across his face. "Would you mind repeating that, please? . . .

"Thank you. Yes, we do know what we're doing, and will you allow me to tell you something in return. In the first place, I am perfectly prepared to take full responsibility for anything that happens. This man Vanin is not to be interfered with at all. When the time is ripe, we'll pull him in, but not till then. Not till I say so, in fact, Mr. Gore-Williams.

"Secondly, I am not in the habit of taking advice from amateurs, whatever their position. I've sat in this chair for a good many years, and I intend to go on sitting here—long after you've been forcibly retired or driven out of office." He pressed the switch of the intercom, and leaned back, grinning at his secretary.

"That's telling the blighter, eh, Florrie?" he said. "Give these halfpenny politicians a yard of rope and they start to imagine it's they, not the departments, who run this blasted country." He released the switch, and all at once his grin vanished.

"What's that you said? Scotland Yard told you—" Kirk listened for a moment and then swung round in his chair.

"Florrie, get through to the Special Branch at once. They've had a phone call tipping them off about Vanin. Sending a squad car to pick him up; Victoria Station at three-thirty; almost that now. Interfering flat-footed fools! They didn't bother to inform us, but told that half-witted sheep Gore-Williams all about it. Damn them!" His hand whitened as it gripped the arm of his chair.

"And we've got to stop that car, Florrie. Whatever happens, Vanin must not be arrested till I give the word." He watched as the girl started to dial the number, and then looked up with a jerk as a voice rang across the desk: an angry, strangled voice that sounded as though its owner were in the last stages of apoplexy.

"What's that, Minister?" Kirk said, noting without concern that the intercom was still connected.

"Oh, did I call you *a half-witted sheep* just now? Sorry about it; heat of the moment and all that. Call me one back, if it makes you feel any better. As it happens, you would be quite justified at the moment." He switched off the set, and leaned back, staring up at the big electric clock on the wall.

Three twenty-six! Unless they could stop that car—unless Vanin was not merely a professional, but an expert—this would be the finish, and they would never hear the end of the story. Kirk knew a good deal about the way M.V.D. agents faced arrest, and there could be only one end. Peter Vanin would be dead.

CHAPTER X

Train announcements and carols creaking hoarsely from the loudspeakers, a lighted tree glowing before the suburban booking office, and three drunks singing their way towards the buffet. A general atmosphere of smoke, gloom, and merriment, and the howl of a locomotive blowing off steam in the Continental arrival bay: Victoria Station on Christmas Eve.

Vanin paid off his taxi, somehow getting great pleasure

from the man's cheerful "Merry Christmas," and shouldered his way through the homegoing crowds. Big crowds, because most of the offices had closed at lunchtime, and the rush to freedom had already started. Crowds with a certain gaiety about them, almost an air of fiesta. He was surprised to see so many smiles on those stolid British faces.

As arranged, Michael Arabin was waiting for him near the clock, and he wore the same dark city suit as before, though now he had a bunch of bright flowers under his arm. There was still that slightly bewildered expression on his face, as though he wasn't sure which card life would turn up next, but his manner was quite different. He seemed trusting and friendly, as though hostility, like a disease, had left him. He held out his hand to Vanin without hesitation.

"Well, I see that you came prepared." Vanin smiled down at the bunch of flowers. "You gave Rolfe my message?"

"Yes, I've carried out my part of the bargain, Mr. Vanin. Just as you told me to. I told him I'd had an anonymous phone call, and gave him the message exactly as you repeated it to me: that he was to be at his house near Cambridge this evening and you would call on him. He didn't say very much to me, but he'll see you, all right. I'm quite certain about that. By the way, here's the address—take you about two hours by car. I've put down the directions."

"Thanks."

Vanin glanced at the slip of paper and pushed it into his pocket. "And how did he react?"

"I don't know—not really. On the surface he seemed quite calm. He just listened to what I said and nodded, as though he were making a purely routine business appointment. I honestly think that during the last few weeks the poor devil has burnt up most of his emotions. As I told you before, I never liked him, but I'm very sorry for him now.

"All the same—" a slight smile flicked across Arabin's face—"when you get there, I wouldn't be at all surprised if he doesn't try to kill you."

"Thanks for telling me—thanks very much indeed." Vanin grinned back at him.

"Now, what about your family? You've checked that they were on the plane all right?"

"Oh, I did that all right. I rang up B.E.A. before I spoke to Rolfe. They should have landed at Gatwick Airport about an hour ago. The connecting train is due here at half past. Yes, for once a Russian seems to have kept a promise, and I'm very grateful to you. I didn't really expect it." Arabin glanced up at the big, soot-encrusted clock as he spoke, and there was suddenly an odd look of embarrassment on his face.

"Look, Mr. Vanin—when we first met, you bought me two drinks which I didn't want. Well, now I'd like to buy you one back. I'd like that very much indeed."

"Thank you. So would I." Vanin smiled with genuine pleasure. "You've got twelve minutes before your train, so let's go." He turned, and together they walked towards the buffet.

The long dreary bar was crowded, but pleasantly crowded. Almost every face had a smile. Vanin looked at the piles of luggage and parcels round each family group: toys for the children, a plant for the widowed sister, sweets and tobacco for some usually neglected grandparent—good will at least once a year, a pleasant family time. Suddenly the thought of his own family was horribly close to him. He pushed it out of his mind as Arabin came back from the counter with glasses in his hands.

"Well, Mr. Vanin," he said. "A very merry Christmas to you. Though I suppose you don't believe in it."

"No, I don't believe in it—not in its truth, that is. All the same, I like the story and the idea behind it. I like them very much indeed." Vanin raised his glass. "Yes, a merry Christmas," he said. "To you and all your family." Behind his back, the drunks he had noticed earlier burst into a loud and tuneless rendering of *Silent Night.*

"Thank you; then here's to both of us." Arabin finished his drink in a single quick movement, and set down the glass on a table beside him. Once again that oddly embarrassed expression flickered across his face.

"Mr. Vanin," he said slowly, "in a way, you're my benefactor, aren't you? You kept your promise and, as I said, I'm grateful. That's why I wondered if you would like to come and meet my family. I'd appreciate it very much if you would."

And Vanin should have known, of course. He'd been a long time in his job, and he should have seen exactly what that look in Arabin's face really meant. He should have got out while the going was good. He wasn't a fool—he should have known.

But he didn't see, and he didn't know. He just stood there with a look of stupid, amateurish pleasure in his eyes, listening to the singing drunks and smiling at Arabin.

"Thank you," he said. "I'd like to meet your family very much. And perhaps we'd better go now. It must be almost time." He glanced at his watch, and finished the drink.

Like the buffet, the platform was very crowded, with happy groups stretched along it waiting for friends and relatives. It was the second platform from the end of the station, and the next one to it, separated by the lines of track, was left open without a barrier. It seemed to be used as a loading bay, with cars and lorries parked alongside. Arabin bought two tickets from the machine and spoke to the man at the gate.

"Yes, this is ours all right, and it seems they'll be at the end of the train—Car 9." He hurried forward, watching the line of numbers strung above the platform. From somewhere in front of them a bell rang, announcing the approaching train.

"This should be it, I think." Arabin stopped and looked down at his bunch of flowers, as though making sure they hadn't been broken or disarranged. Then he raised his eyes and smiled.

"Well, Mr. Vanin," he said. "We're quits, aren't we? We've both kept our promise. We don't owe each other anything."

"Yes, we're quits, but what about it?" As he looked at Arabin's face, a nerve in Vanin's forehead started to tick like a warning light.

"I thought I'd like to mention it for the record, that's all. I gave you certain information to work on, didn't I? I betrayed my employer, and I helped you to injure the country which gave me a home. And in return for that, you released my family—a perfectly fair business arrangement, with no hard feelings on either side." Arabin drew back slightly as he spoke.

"Yes, we're quits, Mr. Vanin. You and I are, that is. But our countries are not quits. Our countries never can be after what you did to us. So, though there's nothing personal in this, I've got a Christmas present for you—a present from Hungary." Without another word he turned on his heel and walked away. In the distance, the little green dot which was the train came sliding down the rails towards the platform.

The three men moved in, one from the front, one from either side, and Vanin knew them—at the first glance he knew them. There was *copper* written all over those heavy, respectable faces, the trilby hats, and the belted raincoats. He drew back slightly towards the very edge of the platform, feeling no bitterness towards Arabin, but utter disgust with himself.

"You fool," he thought. "You poor, incompetent, sentimental failure." For a moment he considered reaching for the little gun in his pocket, and then he knew it was useless. These men were professionals like himself. They would have him before his hand was halfway there. Only the thing in his mouth seemed real and powerful.

"Mr. Vanin?" The voice was pleasant and polite, because it wasn't sure of itself yet. They were acting without real information at the moment; merely on what Arabin had told them on the phone. With a little more evidence behind it, Vanin sensed that the voice would sound very different.

"Would you mind coming with us, sir? We are police officers and have one or two questions to ask you." To their right, the train clicked over the points and began to run into the station.

"Yes, gentlemen, of course I'll come with you." Vanin smiled pleasantly and moved his tongue, feeling the little capsule slide up into position. It seemed hard and firm, but he knew that one good grip with his teeth would break it open. About ten seconds it would take, he supposed. Just ten seconds, and then a single sharp pain and all would be over. Very easy and pleasant, really; no more worry, no more fear. If only it wasn't for Shura and the kids. At the thought, he released the capsule and felt it slide back to safety. Behind his back came the grinding of braked wheels.

"No—" he said, still smiling at the policemen, judging the distance, and knowing that he had about one chance in a hundred left to him, but also knowing that he had to take it. That the book required him to take it, and he always went by the book. "No, I'm damned if I'll come with you." He braced his body and flung himself sideways in front of the train.

And he very nearly made it. He felt fingers tearing at his sleeve and letting go. He heard a woman screaming, as his feet left the platform. He felt his feet catch on a rail and throw him forward. Then there was suddenly nothing, except the roar of the train with its bulk looming over him, and the chassis coming at him like a battering ram, and the wheels running towards his legs like knives. For one second he seemed to see the driver's face looking down at him, as though from the top of a high building—and then he was past it.

He was past the chassis, and the coupling and wheels, with his feet scrabbling on the ballast towards the next track and the next platform—the platform without a barrier. For a moment he felt he had made it, and then he didn't feel anything except pain. Great waves of pain flowing over him, while something like an iron hand picked him up, carried him forward, and then threw him aside as a child throws away a broken doll.

He lay beneath the lip of the platform, with consciousness coming back and pain urging it on. Though it felt like a lifetime since the buffer had caught him, it could only have been seconds, for behind his back on the next track the train was still moving. As though it were the last thing he would ever do, he pulled himself upright, and started to climb onto the platform.

Mercifully, it was deserted. He looked around him for a moment, and then crawled forward between the shelter of the parked vans, feeling the edges of broken bones grinding like files in his chest. Two ribs gone, he decided, maybe three; still, he was alive. He had a chance of getting away, and there were worse things than broken bones. He fought back nausea, and half ran, half staggered out of the station.

And his luck was holding out. As he reached the pavement, a bus was just starting to pull away. He hurled himself at it, his right hand clutching the pillar and his feet dragging wildly in the gutter. It took every ounce of strength to pull himself on board.

"Easy, thar—jest watch it." The Negro conductor scowled, and yelped with pain and annoyance as Vanin's body cannoned against his.

"That was a stoopid thing to do, sah; boardin' a bus when she's in motion. Jest you look what it says here." He pointed pompously at a notice on the panel. *"It is an offence for any passenger to—"*

"I'm very sorry, conductor." Vanin twisted his face into an apologetic grin and fought back his terrible desire to vomit. "I'm a foreigner, you see, and I don't understand all your regulations. Besides I was in a great hurry. Would you give me a sixpenny ticket, please." He reached in his pocket for the coin.

"Well, I dunno about that." The black potentate, after the first shock, was obviously starting to enjoy himself. "Very dangerous thing you done then, gettin' on when we'se a' movin'. Right against regulations too. Under the circumstances I'd be quite justified in turning you off mah bus." His hand moved towards the bell as he spoke.

"'Gainst regulations indeed!" A stout lady whose parcels seemed to cover most of the back seat came quickly to Vanin's rescue. "And you're a fine one to talk about regulations, conductor!" Her voice was loud and ringing and addressed as much to her fellow passengers as to the Negro.

"Yes, we know all about you busmen, don't we?" she continued. "Crawlin' about in convoys to save yourselves work, and keeping people waiting—goin' on strike when you feel like it, and making my old man cycle to work, and him a martyr to rheumatism—pullin' away from the curb, when you see somebody trying to catch the bus. Oh, yes, I saw what happened, conductor. You rang yer bell too soon, and I wouldn't blame this gentleman if he doesn't take yer to court. What's more, if you don't give him his ticket at once, I'll put in a report to the next inspector we come across." She leaned forward with a glow of malicious pleasure in her eyes. "That's right, Number 87505, give 'im his ticket, or I'll shop yer." She turned a motherly smile on Vanin, as the Negro beat a hasty retreat to the upper deck.

"Now, you come and sit down by me, sir. Nasty shaking up you've had just then. I saw the brute ring 'is bell when you was coming across the pavement. . . . A foreigner too, are you? Well, at least you 'ave the decency to admit it; not like some. What the hell do these bloody Jamaicans think they are?" Though the bus was half empty, a loud murmur of approval greeted her words.

"Thank you, madam. Thank you very much indeed. You are very kind." Vanin raised his hat and bowed slightly. "If you don't mind, I'll stand here for a little—rather winded, you see." He stared out through the rear window of the bus. Far back in the line of crawling traffic a black car was trying to overtake a lorry, and he heard a sound which might have been a police bell. At the same moment, the bus stopped again, and he saw the welcome sight of an underground station.

"Thank you," he said to the stout lady who had probably saved his life. "Thank you once again." He dropped off the bus and walked towards the station.

He ran all the way down the escalator steps, and it was like a descent into Hell; his pain was localized now. A sharp, biting pain in his chest as though an animal were tearing at the flesh. Somehow he made it, though, and from now on he vowed he would take no more chances. Three times he changed trains, and at each station he looked carefully around him. Only when he was certain he had not been followed did he think of his body. He walked into a lavatory and inspected the damage.

Yes, it seemed that there were just a couple of ribs gone and he was in no immediate danger. The fractures had bent outwards, tearing at the skin but keeping clear of the lungs and arteries. If only the pain would stop he could keep going a long time. If only he had some morphia or even a drink to help him. Yes, that was it—a drink. The thought of alcohol was suddenly like a spar floating towards a drowning sailor. He had to have a drink or he'd pass out. He tightened his coat, and staggered out of the lavatory towards a sign reading LIFTS & EXIT.

Apart from a small, harassed-looking man with an evening paper held out in front of him, Vanin was alone in the lift cage, and if his thoughts hadn't been elsewhere, the paper might have amused him slightly. It was open with the financial page turned towards him and the headlines read, WILL WE FILL OUR STOCKINGS AFTER CHRISTMAS THIS YEAR? LORD TREMAYNE'S VISIT TO WASHINGTON.

But Vanin was not interested in his mission any more. Only pain interested him now. He stepped out of the station, standing in the entrance for a moment and looking for the thing that could keep him going. He was in an area of narrow, crowded streets and small shops, and just at the corner nearby stood a public house. Very slowly he started to move towards it, his breath misting in the thin, frozen air and the knives in his chest grinding at every step. Even as his hand reached for the door of the bar he knew it was useless, and felt the lock hold against him.

No, no, this might be Christmas Eve, but there was no drink or comfort for him—no alcohol when he really needed it. When he needed it for the first time in his life. He cursed the British licencing laws, and stumbled deeper into Soho. The bars were shut, but there might be a chemist who would help him. Yes, if he played his cards right, a chemist might give him something.

"Hullo, darling. You looking for a good time?" The girl, or woman rather, stood in a doorway and though the temperature was well under freezing she seemed to be wearing nothing except a tight black dress. Her face was bloated with cold and her smile was hard and automatic. To Vanin it seemed the kindest, warmest smile that he had ever looked at.

"A good time? That depends what you mean, doesn't it? If there's a drink going I'd like it. I'd like that very much indeed."

"A drink, darling!" The woman frowned slightly, looking at his face and the sway of his body. "Are you sure you haven't had enough already?" She squeezed her face back into its professional mask of welcome.

"All the same, why not?" she said, considering. "It's Christmas Eve, isn't it? Everybody must have a little drink on Christmas Eve. Come on down and join our party. Plenty to drink, and lots of little girls looking for a nice friend. Warm too." She shivered slightly and took his arm.

The *party* was a sad Maltese waiter behind a tiny bar, a manageress who said she had seen better days, three young whores from the Midlands, and a boy named Patrick Jesus Murphy who imagined he was tough. They smiled in different ways as Vanin came into the room. The waiter humbly, the women as though they were seeing the sea for the first time, Mr. Murphy toughly: the grin of the killer in the Western saloon—Jack Palance looking at his target. The grin didn't quite come off. There were nine generations of bad food, bad housing, and consumption behind it.

The manageress greeted him. "Good afternoon, sir. Now, just you sit down and make yourself comfortable. We're all friends here." She fussed round him, seeing "drunk" and "sucker" in every inch of his body.

"As it's Christmas," she added, "what about buying a drink for the house?"

"The house? Oh, yes, of course; I'd be delighted." Vanin glanced round the room. It was dominated by an enormous scarlet juke box, and photographs of film stars covered the walls.

"Would you make mine whiskey, please," he said. "A large one with no water or soda."

"Whiskey, sir! Oh, I'm very sorry, but with the Christmas rush, we're right out of whiskey." She gave the waiter a sideways grin and he busied himself at the bar. "We've got something else though—something very nice indeed. It's our own speciality, and you'll enjoy it all right, sir."

"Very well, anything you've got, so long as it's strong." Vanin leaned back in his chair, seeing the woman who had accosted him outside sit down beside him and arch forward. Her dress was cut very low and there was a little pinkish mole between her breasts.

"You feeling all right now, darling?" she said. "Not feeling sick, are you? When I saw you in the street, I thought you might—"

"No, no, I'm all right." Vanin shook his head, and smiled as the waiter set two glasses of purple-coloured liquid before them. "Just thirsty, that's all."

He knew what kind of place this was, all right. Moscow was getting full of joints just like it. The police closed them down every so often, but they always managed to start up again elsewhere. Supply and demand, he thought sadly. In his case the demand was purely for alcohol. The only woman he wanted was a little matchstick drawing invented by John Flack.

But at least the drink would be strong—strong and fiery. He could promise himself that. Probably liable to cause blindness if taken in any quantity. What did they call it at home? Yes, "Momma Sophie," a home-brewed and very raw form of Schnapps—just what he needed in his present situation. He held the glass in his hand, but he didn't drink at once. He wanted to hang onto pain, knowing that in a few seconds it would be dulled. He was an abstemious man, and his stomach was empty. This stuff should work quickly. He pulled out his wallet and handed the waiter a five-pound note, quite oblivious of the eyes watching him. From across the room the juke box started to grind out a carol.

"Once in Royal David's city—Stood a lonely cattle shed." He giggled foolishly at the words, and smiled at the girl beside him.

"I was born in a shed," he said, remembering what his mother had told him: a shack near Archangel, with the Red, White, and British armies fighting it out over the putrid snow.

"In a shed! You are a one, darling. Don't be so silly, though. Nobody is born in a shed these days." She smiled back and raised her glass. "Anyway drink up and let's have another round. Plenty more where this comes from. And a happy Christmas, darling. A happy Christmas to everybody."

"Yes, a happy Christmas." He raised his own glass and brought it slowly to his lips. This was what he had come for—what he wanted. The thing that could deaden pain. He tilted his head and drank deeply.

Oh, no! Oh, dear God, no! Oh, please let me be wrong! The glass came down in his hand to spill on the table, and he knew that he wasn't wrong; that he hadn't make a mistake. There was no power in the stuff at all, not a trace of alcohol. It was just like drinking soapy water with a slight taste of fruit juice. He looked wildly around him, knowing that within seconds he had to be sick. Ignoring the girl's cry as the liquid slopped over her dress, he staggered towards a door at the corner of the room.

The door was marked TOILETS and it led into a long, dark passage smelling of cats, overcooked greens, and garbage. At the end of it were three more rooms, one running out into a yard and the others labelled HIS and HERS in heraldic lettering.

HIS was a gloomy little room, laid with dirty grey lino and containing two urinals, a cubicle, and a washbasin that was almost overflowing with cigarette ends. Vanin lurched into the cubicle and did what he had to do. He did it with closed eyes, and nausea as strong as the pain in his body. When he had finished he felt better, but not much better. He straightened from the pan and started to wipe his mouth. As he did so, he noticed the writings and drawings on the walls, and he smiled slightly in spite of the pain. On the surface, the English seemed a sane, commonplace people, but their lavatories belied them: hardly a sexual perversion had been left unrecorded. He pulled the chain, and moved across to the washbasin. Though it was choked with rubbish, at least the tap worked. He had started to sluice his face when footsteps sounded in the passage and the door opened.

"Okay, feller, let's have it, shall we? Let's just see that roll in your pocket." The boy called Murphy came into the room nice and slow and easy, as the cinema and the television had taught him, but he still looked what he was—a punk and quite harmless. Even though he thought he was going to rob a drunk, even with the knife in his hand, he looked harmless. It wasn't just a flick knife that he held either, but a *genuine, hollow-ground, imported, Italian stiletto; useful for hunting and self-defence,* as advertised in the *Confidential Detective Magazine*—thirty-five cents in the States, one shilling and sixpence in England. Murphy raised it slightly and began to walk towards Vanin.

"Yes, boy, I saw that roll of fivers in your wallet, so let's have it. Let's have it quickly. This baby in my hand hasn't had a drink in days, and she's getting thirsty. Do you want I should give her some of your blood to drink?" His voice was just right: hard, and cold, and cynical. A very large percentage of the entertainment industry had been paid to train it the way it was.

"Come on and be quick about it," the boy said. "Hand over, you bloody foreigner."

"All right, just take it easy, son. You can have my wallet—you can have all I've got." Vanin twisted his face into a drunken grin. The sickness had cleared his mind again and he was almost starting to enjoy himself. Though he worked to destroy their system, he still liked the British as a people. It would be pleasant to rid them of a very nasty parasite. Besides, in a way he was a policeman himself. It was part of the job.

"Yes, take my money—plenty more where it came from. Take all I've got, but please put your knife away." He giggled foolishly and reached in his pocket, feeling his fingers tighten round the fountain pen: the little, shining charm that warded off evil.

"And take this too, if you want. It's a very nice pen if you know how to use it; probably cost more to make than you could earn in a year." As he looked at the boy's face, Vanin knew that whatever he offered him, Murphy would still use that knife—it was almost a part of him. What the boy did was as much for pleasure as for gain, though gain was important. This was going to be a good day for Murphy: a wallet full of fivers, a valuable fountain pen, and a drunk to be slashed. What more could one want in life?

But all the same, Vanin couldn't kill him after all. Whatever the book said, however strong his loathing, he couldn't kill him. Vanin was a professional and he wasn't paid to kill louts or children. Still he would leave behind something to be remembered by.

"All right, son," he said, "let's just see if you can take me." His voice was quite different now, without a trace of alcohol in it. "Your police couldn't an hour ago, so let's find out how good you are. Come and get me, if you think you can. . . . Very well, if that's how you want it."

He watched the tense, hating body start to spring forward, saw the knife glitter under the light bulb; then Vanin's fingers pressed the catch of the pen. As it had done before, the little gun jumped three times with hardly a sound. For a moment Vanin stood looking down at his handiwork; then he walked out towards the yard.

He had struck a blow for law and order, and he was pleased with himself, for he was a policeman. As far as crime was concerned, Mr. Murphy was now a back number who would never pull a knife on anybody again: he wouldn't even be able to hold a knife. When the doctors cleaned him up, they would find that Mr. Murphy had lost his right hand.

CHAPTER XI

"Arabin—Michael Arabin? No, General Kirk, I don't think Vanin ever mentioned him to me, though he said he had an appointment with somebody this afternoon. . . . I see." Kate bent over the phone that had belonged to the real Miss Reilly, and a little spasm of pain flitted across her forehead. "So that means it's all finished, as far as we're concerned, sir. The police were tipped off to meet Vanin at Victoria Station, and he'll either be dead or under arrest by now."

Her eyes studied the room as she spoke. It was a very bare room, without decoration except for its late owner's pictures hanging from the walls. There were a great many pictures, with different subject matter, but the treatment of each was similar, and it showed despair. A jagged mountain rising up out of the mist, its flanks and summit underlined with black paint—a stunted tree with oddly claw-like branches stretching out across a bare moorland—a ruined cottage hanging from a cliff face. There was only moderate talent in the pictures, but they told a good deal about the artist's psychology.

And just in front of her, above the fireplace, was a scene she recognized: the three crosses at Mizzen Head, where she had first met Vanin. She would remember that meeting till her dying day: the fog, the roar of the signal gun from the lighthouse, and here and there the vague outlines of grazing sheep. She had waited a long time behind that Calvary, wondering and dreading what kind of man she was going to meet. It was her first mission of this kind, and fear had been as thick as the mist around her.

Then, up the path from the sea, she had heard footsteps and seen the man come out through the mist and walk towards the line of crosses. As he gave the passwords, his voice had sounded quite different from what she had expected—low, and gentle, and anxious. She suddenly knew that there was nothing to worry about, for this man was as frightened as she was, and her own fear had left her. *"Lord, remember me when thou comest into thy Kingdom."* She had felt great warmth for Vanin as she listened to those words.

"No, my girl, it's not finished, not by a long chalk." Kirk's voice on the phone brought her back to the present with a jerk.

"It seems," Kirk went on, "that Mr. Vanin knew his job, and was a bit too quick for our friends in blue. This fellow Arabin did his stuff all right—took Vanin onto the platform as arranged—and everything was set for the bobbies to pick him up. Then, when they tried to do so, he took off; chucked himself in front of a train. The fools! The damned interfering fools! Just why couldn't they contact us before sending that car?"

"I see, sir. Then that means—" Once again the little tic ran across Kate's forehead.

"I'm afraid it doesn't mean anything, my dear. Vanin wasn't killed, you see. The wretched fellow appears to have the lives of a cat. He managed to make it in front of that train, climbed up onto the next-door platform, and got away scot-free. Now he's on the loose, and he'll know we're after him. Yes, Mr. Vanin has shown himself quite a bright boy, and it'll be the devil of a job to pick him up—probably on his way back to Russia by now." Kirk was in a vile temper, and the connection was poor. His voice sounded like a blunt saw hacking its way through soft timber.

"No, I don't think he'll do that, sir—not yet." Kate concentrated on what she knew about Vanin. "I've got the impression that he was told to finish this assignment whatever happens. He's got a family in Russia, and he seemed to imply that there might be reprisals against them if he failed."

"I see. Yes, that's a common enough practice of Malendin's, by all accounts. And let's just hope you're right. If we don't pick him up, there'll be the devil to pay. Now for the future.

I'll have to put out a general call for Vanin, and publish that picture you took for me. All the same, I don't think we'll get him in a hurry—not unless he contacts you again. There's nothing else you can tell me, is there? Only what he said about this baby of Rolfe's?"

"That's right, sir. He said he'd get in touch with me if anything went wrong, but it wasn't likely."

"Very well. Then we'll just have to wait and see. I'll put out some feelers towards Martin Rolfe, and you sit tight and pray that Vanin does get in touch with you. Goodbye for the present, my dear."

"Goodbye, General." She dropped the phone back onto its rest, and glanced at the little hurrying clock on the mantelpiece: nearly five o'clock, and Christmas had started. Through the uncurtained windows, cars and buses lurched on towards the suburbs and home. Home! Home to the family—home to friends—home for Christmas! Everybody going home except one little man who had to finish his job and work late. Peter Vanin with the world against him, trying to find the answer to something that happened a long time ago—something to do with a child that was murdered twenty years ago.

She got up from her chair by the telephone and crossed to the fire, warming her hands and then lighting a cigarette to steady her nerves. As she did so, she suddenly heard the footsteps: slow, heavy—terribly heavy—footsteps, coming across the landing outside. A moment later the doorbell started to ring.

The bell rang and rang without pause, as though something was wedged against it, but Kate didn't answer it at once. She stood still, staring in front of her and knowing that she'd been wrong just now—terribly wrong. The whole world wasn't against Vanin. He had friends, all right, and one of them might be outside that door now. A friend who probably knew the real Kate Reilly; an unpleasant friend who would know how to deal with a spy.

All the same, she put down her cigarette and crossed to the

door. Whoever was outside had to be answered. She reached for the Yale handle, hearing the bell like a pain in her head and feeling the lock stiff and heavy, as though a great weight were pressed against it. She pulled harder. Suddenly the door opened with a jerk that threw her sideways, and Peter Vanin fell at her feet.

Vanin looked up at her from his knees, and he didn't say anything at all. For perhaps five seconds he crouched like that and his eyes swept round the room as though looking for something that had been hidden there and forgotten. Then he started to crawl towards a cabinet by the window. The brandy bottle was a quarter empty when he put it down and pulled himself to his feet.

"I'm sorry, my dear," he said at last, and it was like a corpse speaking. "I really am terribly sorry. I have no right to come here, but it seemed the only place. I don't think I was followed, though." He glanced out through the window and pulled the curtains closed. With the brandy, a little colour was coming into his face.

"It's all right, Peter. It's quite all right." Kate came towards him staring at the lines under his eyes and the odd tilt of his body. "But you're hurt, aren't you? That train did get you when you jumped—" She broke off, cursing her own stupidity.

"Yes, it got me all right—got me here." He ran his hand across his chest and there was no suspicion in his eyes—only curiosity and pain. "But how did you know about the train?"

"Oh, it was on the radio just now." Once she had recovered herself the lie came easily. "They said that a man suspected of being an enemy agent had escaped by jumping in front of a train at Victoria; they described him. I thought it had to be you."

"I see. They're quick off the mark, aren't they?" Vanin leaned back against the cabinet, as though unsure of his legs.

"Yes, it was me all right," he said wearily. "I had to pay the price of a very foolish action, and the buffer of the train got me here. Nothing too serious, but I think I've smashed a couple of ribs. Give me a hand, will you? Thanks." He shuddered slightly as she helped him off with the coat and unbuttoned his shirt. His chest was thin and almost hairless, and very white—except for one place. A little below the left armpit there was a great purple swelling like a growth.

"You've broken two ribs." At the moment all thoughts of Kirk and her job had left Kate and she was a primitive creature: a woman trying to help an injured man she had grown fond of. Her fingers ran across the swelling, feeling splintered bone beneath the flesh. "They're badly broken too, Peter. I couldn't set them in a hundred years. We'll have to get a doctor somehow."

"No, no doctor, Kate. I haven't got time for that." Vanin glanced at the clock above the mantelpiece. "I dare say our friend Tanek could provide a doctor if we asked him, but there's no time. I've got an appointment very soon, and I must keep it." He took the cigarette she lit for him and dragged hard at it. Even with brandy his face was much the same colour as the smoke.

"No," he went on, "you'll just have to try and fix me up as best you can. You said you've been a nurse, so get to work. Just tie me up so these ribs don't move any more. Tear up a sheet if you haven't got a bandage. It needn't be a good job, but try and make me hold together for a few more hours. After that it doesn't matter what happens—nothing will matter. In about four hours I'll have done what I was told to do, and Shura will be—"

"Shura? Shura's your wife, isn't she?" Kate folded the wad of lint and undid the roll of elastic she had found in a drawer. All at once the larger job didn't seem important to her—nothing seemed important except this man with his broken body, and she remembered again her thoughts in Kirk's office: *I won't underrate him, but I might get fond of him.*

"Yes, Shura's my wife. I've got two children as well, a boy and a little girl. If I do what I'm paid to do, Malendin will see that they're looked after; also if I fail but manage to die heroically." He grinned, and then shuddered with pain as Kate started to pull on the bandage. As it tightened she felt the ribs draw back into position. There was a sudden longing in her eyes as she looked at his body, though it wasn't much to look at: lean and white and broken, but still vital—terribly vital. Every bit of it from the thin shoes to the Slavic face with the lines under its eyes was vital. If it hadn't been for Shura, Kate might have betrayed her country for Peter Vanin's body.

"Ah, that's much better," said Vanin. He watched her pin the bandage, and flexed his arm. "Yes, I feel a new man already. This should hold me in one piece for quite a time." He started to pull back his shirt. "Now there's just one more thing I need from you, and then I won't trouble you again. I think you said you have a car in London.... Good, then I'm afraid I must borrow it for a while."

Once again he smiled. "Don't worry though. I'll remember to drive on the proper side of the road, and you'll get it back all right. Just report it as stolen in the morning."

"Yes, of course." Kate reached in her bag and handed him the keys. "It's a blue Lancia, parked outside, and the number's on this fob." She watched him straighten his tie, and for a second her fingers brushed against his arm.

"Peter," she said, and she felt like a Judas to both sides as she said it. "Peter, why don't you give up? Nobody could blame you, you know, and you haven't got a chance. They'll have your picture in the papers, and someone's bound to recognize you. Why not get out while you can? There's certain to be a Russian steamer in the docks, and if you went now you might just make it. Please, Peter, I know what I'm talking about."

But Vanin wasn't even listening. His tie was quite straight now and he started to put on his hat. He might not have been in the same room. Love and hatred were very close to Kate.

"All right then, Comrade Vanin," she said. "Go and die if you have to, but play it fair. Just tell me where you're going and what is this important appointment. What is the story of the Rolfe baby? You owe me that much, I think."

"Very well, you can have it." He crossed to the mirror and looked at himself: a junior executive preparing for an important client.

"I'm going to see somebody about a child," he said. "A little dead child who can bring down the economy of this country like a pack of cards. Here's a letter giving all the details—everything I know. You can read it if you want, but be sure Tanek gets it in the morning. One of his people will have to take over when I've prepared the ground."

He handed her the envelope and stood staring at her for a moment. She was a very beautiful woman, but she didn't mean anything to him—hardly anything. All the same her lips were warm and friendly, and he needed friendship; he needed that more than anything in the world. For a second his lips met hers, holding them as though they were the last things he would ever touch, and feeling her body respond. Then, very gently, he pushed her away.

"No, my dear," he said. "I'm sorry, but it's too late now—far too late. Once we might have been good for each other, but not now. Now I wouldn't be good for anyone. Now I'm just a poor, bloody cripple who stinks of death. Also I have an appointment to keep." He turned and walked across to the door, resting his hand on the knob. Just before he pulled it open, he looked back at her, bringing his eyes slowly up from the floor to her face, and taking in every curve of her body. Kate had never felt more naked than she did under those vital eyes.

"Goodbye, my dear," he said very quietly, "and thanks for everything. Maybe we will meet again one day, and then—" He shook his head and smiled.

Then he added: "But what a waste it's been—what a terrible waste, my lovely, hungry, little Irish girl."

Like the last page of a book closing, the door shut behind him and Kate was alone. For a long moment she stared at the door, and then she tore open the envelope in her hand and crossed to the telephone. Her fingers felt as though they were turning an enormous wheel as she dialled Kirk's number.

CHAPTER XII

Vanin drove fast out of London, but not too fast. Though he had studied the map before he started, the English roads were difficult to distinguish by night and he didn't want any police car to stop him for speeding. He crawled on through Hammersmith, and Chiswick, and the sprawling wilderness of the South Circular Road—uniform houses and little factories, railway bridges and filling stations. Drive for perhaps a mile and then stop at the traffic lights, wait five minutes and crawl on again.

But at last he was through the heavy traffic pouring out of London, and he put his foot down, revelling in the low whine of the engine, which seemed to remain constant from walking pace to eighty. The Lancia was by far the finest car he had ever driven and he envied Kate its possession, thinking of his own battered and ancient Zis. Some of these foreign agents were paid very good money, it seemed. Far better than anything the home staff could expect.

The bandage was holding well, and the dull ache in his chest hardly troubled him. If the need arose he could rely on his body working efficiently. All the same, the effects of the brandy were beginning to wear off, and there was a stale, strangely metallic taste in his mouth. Also, he was in for one of the most difficult evenings in his life: if things went wrong, it could be his last evening, and he needed help. He pulled the car up before a little public house outside Cambridge and went in, hoping for Dutch courage.

"And why *Dutch?*" he wondered, standing at the bar and smiling around him. He was interested in the formation of words, and the idiosyncrasies of English amused him.

Yes, Dutch courage, a Dutch uncle, a Dutch treat—not

to mention Spanish fly and French letters. All slightly reprehensible things. A very strange and insular people, the British, he thought, looking at the hearty faces almost filling the room, though it was Christmas Eve and they were allowed to drink till midnight. The British were tolerant enough, but had a strange contempt for everything foreign.

A rich, happy people too, at the moment—but only at the moment. If his theory was correct—if Rolfe broke and gave the wrong answers at that Washington conference—they wouldn't be rich much longer. Before another Christmas came round, there might be bread queues in England. The thought saddened him slightly, and he finished his drink and went out.

Flat country now, though the road still twisted and turned in respect for ancient property rights. Flat, wide fields stretching away before him under the bright wintry moon, which almost made his headlights unnecessary. And, as Arabin had said, there were few houses but many churches: great, towering churches dominating every little slope and standing out like sails on the horizon. He remembered that this had once been a populous area, till the wool trade moved away. The people had gone now, the houses had fallen down and decayed, but the churches remained: empty monuments to a former greatness.

An endless countryside, too. The sea could only have been a few miles away, but the land looked as though it would stretch on forever. Somehow it reminded him of the Russian steppes.

And he was nearly there now. He glanced at the dashboard clock as a signpost slid past him and he turned the car up a little lane to his right. Almost eight o'clock and Heronsford three miles away. In a very few minutes he would be standing before the man he had been told to break, the man with a guilty secret which could make him the slave of the M.V.D. for life. Only three miles and Vanin would know if his theory was correct.

The place was just as Arabin had described it to him. A high wall surrounded the grounds, and there was a porter's lodge with a pair of wrought-iron gates beside it. He rang the bell and gave his name to an old man who checked it against a dirty scrap of paper, muttering to himself as he did so. Then the gates were opened and he drove on towards the loom of a big house standing back amongst the trees.

He hadn't far to go, but he took it carefully. The drive was in poor condition, with deep pits and ruts, and there was a heavy frost in the air. His tires slipped and scrabbled on fallen leaves as they mounted the slope, but at last he drew up in front of the house. It looked enormous in the clear winter night, with crazy towers and battlements rising above the roof and not a light showing anywhere. He pulled at a heavy, old-fashioned bell handle in the porch and waited. He waited a long time, but at last a lamp came on through the fanlight and he heard footsteps. Then the door opened and he was looking at the man he had come to destroy.

"Mr. Peter Vanin? You are the person who telephoned my secretary this morning?" Martin Rolfe stood on the step looking down at him, and he was tall—much taller than Vanin had expected. He was thinner too, and his face bore no resemblance to the academic, self-confident mask that had stared out from the walls of Flack's house. His hair was still thick and dark but the flesh below it was the colour and texture of grey paper: the face of a man who slept little and whose few dreams were nightmares.

And yet, as Vanin looked at Martin Rolfe, he knew that this wasn't quite the haunted face he expected. There was sadness in those restless eyes, but somehow no fear. Rolfe looked as though he had walked through the gates of hell and come out with courage intact.

"Yes, my name is Vanin," he said, and stepped past him into the hall. A big, dark hall with chipped oak panelling, and stags' heads and rusty medieval weapons on the walls, and everywhere a slight odour of neglect and decay. The home of a man who was probably worth a million pounds.

To their right a staircase ran up to a landing, and someone was on the landing: a tall woman in a very bright dress staring down at them. Vanin was reminded of Arabin's description of

Lady Rolfe: "Her make-up stood out like sealing wax on an envelope." He suddenly had the uncomfortable feeling that he was entering not a house but a prison.

"Will you please come this way, Mr. Vanin." Rolfe closed the door and led him to a room beyond the stairs. It was a long, narrow room and seemed to be used as part study and part library. There were bookcases along the whole of one wall and at the far end a big red curtain which probably divided it from an adjoining room. To the right of the curtain was a mahogany desk with a portrait of Rolfe hanging behind it. The portrait figure, dressed in scarlet and gold, held some kind of silver baton in his hand and wore a cap with eagle's feathers and fur flaps. It was obviously some form of academic dress, and the Rolfe of the painting made a fine sight as he stood there. Dashing, and gallant, and brave—quite divorced from the grey figure who moved slowly to the desk.

"Well, Mr. Vanin," Rolfe said, somehow managing a smile. "You asked to see me, and here I am. At the moment I know nothing about you, but you claim to know something about me—about a certain event in my life which happened a long time ago. You have written letters to that effect, but have now come into the open. Well, shall we talk business, or do you want to prolong the agony still further?"

"We'll talk business, Sir Martin, and I don't want to cause anybody agony. I am purely a businessman—" Vanin broke off and leaned forward as Rolfe opened a drawer in the desk. "But don't try anything—don't try to do anything silly. I belong to a big organization, and I've left a letter giving all the details I know. If you killed me it would merely mean that someone else took my place."

"If I killed you!" Rolfe's eyebrows came up in a bar across his forehead. "Oh, I see." He closed the drawer again, and there was a short, blackened pipe in his hand.

"You thought I was bringing out a gun, did you?" Rolfe said. "No, I don't imagine that that would do any good, and I'm sure you've written a most comprehensive letter." He filled the pipe very carefully and struck a match. Only when it was drawing to his complete satisfaction did he speak again. "Now, as we agreed, let's talk business. During the last few months you, or some of your friends, have been sending letters which imply that you have certain damaging information against me. Well, you've come into the open, so please sit down and tell me what you think you know, and what you want from me."

"Thank you." Vanin leaned back in the chair and crossed his legs, looking not at Rolfe but at the picture behind him. Somehow not looking at Rolfe made it easier to talk to him.

And Vanin told him everything from the beginning. He told Rolfe who he was, and what the department wanted, and how they had received the first communication from Arabin. He told him about Flack, and how Flack had died, and about the man Julius who died with him. He told him what he had learned from Superintendent Pode, and what Kate had seen in the doctor's notebooks. Then he turned away from the picture and looked at Rolfe himself.

As he did so, he suddenly felt all confidence drain away, and he knew he was wrong—completely wrong. For there was no fear or even acceptance in the man's face. Rolfe's face was as strong and confident as Vanin had seen it in the newspaper cuttings, and it was smiling.

"So, that's it. That's who you are, and what you think you know. That's what you will have put in the letter to your colleagues. You are to be complimented on a fertile imagination, Mr. Vanin; also to be thanked." The pipe had gone out as he listened and Rolfe picked up the matches again.

"Oh, yes, I'm grateful to you, Mr. Vanin; very grateful. You and your assistant killed Flack, and Flack was the only person who could hurt me. It seems that I have nothing more to worry about.

"No, I'm afraid your theory is quite impossible, and there's no need to take my word for it. Just check with the Queen Mary Nursing Home in Chelsea. If the records still exist they'll tell you that for six weeks after her child was born my wife was a very sick woman and in their care. She could no more have taken that pram than you could have done." As though changing his mind, Rolfe pushed the matches back into his pocket and laid down the pipe. "Won't you try and guess what really happened, Mr. Vanin?"

"No, no—I don't need to guess any more." Though Vanin answered him, he had hardly heard Rolfe's last words. He was staring up at the picture again, and this time it told him the whole truth. The painting of a slim man with rather delicate features, dressed in Tudor costume, and the plumed cap on his head with the long fur flaps that framed the face like a woman's hair.

And that was the point, of course—like a woman's hair. That was what Flack must have seen—a reproduction of this portrait—and it had told him the truth. It had made Flack remember what he had actually looked at through the snow in 1940. A tall woman standing outside a shop window, whose face—her man's face—had been almost hidden by flowing hair. That was the only way it could have been, and Flack's words were very clear in Vanin's head: "The Gaunt Woman was born twenty years ago, and she died the same day."

"It was you," he said. "You did it all on your own."

"That's right, Mr. Vanin—all on my own." Rolfe had moved away from the desk and was standing with his back to the curtain.

"You know who the Gaunt Woman was, and my wife never had any idea of how or why her son died. I worked all by myself, and if I may quote from an American marching song, 'I don't want no pardon for anything I've done.'" He was back at his desk and his well-bred, academic voice made the words sound slightly ridiculous. The automatic he held looked like a stage prop in his slender hand.

"All right, Stirling Moss, there's no need to hurry. Just take it nice, and slow, and easy." Kirk leaned forward in the car seat, grumbling at the driver and massaging his hands together as he did so. Though the windows were closed and a heater roared at full blast, his overcoat was tightly buttoned to protect his chest from the treacherous night air. He scowled at the dashboard clock, checked it with his watch, and then turned to Kate and Trubenoff.

"No, I don't think we want to get there too early. Unless a miracle comes up, or our friends the police let us down badly, there's no chance of Vanin slipping through our fingers. If he does, I'll have to start applying for another job without delay.

"It's not Vanin, but Rolfe I'm interested in now. If there really is something on him to make him a potential victim for blackmail, then he's a damn bad security risk, and the Minister will have to get himself another adviser without delay. I want friend Vanin to have plenty of time for his interview, and then I'll be very interested to hear Rolfe's account of it. . . . And here come our reinforcements, I think." Kirk wound down the window as the car drew up before a swinging torch. A uniformed figure walked towards them.

"Ah, there you are, Inspector," said Kirk. "You've seen our man go through all right?"

"That we did, sir. Exactly forty minutes ago it was." The policeman consulted his notebook.

"A blue Lancia saloon it was, registration number AVK 995, driven by a man on his own. No chance of his spotting us, either. I had two constables hidden in the bushes where the lane joins the main road."

"Good. And you've got the place surrounded, as I asked?"

"Yes, sir. I put my men in ten minutes after he passed. There's no chance of his getting away from us—not without a miracle, that is."

"Um, well, don't be too confident about that. This joker has proved himself to be quite a miracle worker." Kirk grunted slightly. "Just keep your wits about you, and remember he's armed. Shoot if you have to, but only to cripple him. We'll start to move in five minutes."

Kirk wound up his window and stared at the clock again. Not one of them spoke as they waited, and its hurrying minute hand seemed the only living thing in their little warm world. Then Kirk adjusted his collar and leaned forward.

"All right, children," he said. "Let's go, shall we? And this time it's got to be for the kill."

CHAPTER XIII

"Yes, that's right, Mr. Vanin, I did it. All on my own I did it." Expressionless, Rolfe stood against the curtain.

"I made the decision. I did what I had to do, and I've no regrets. It wasn't really difficult, either. I was slim in those days, and I'd always been a good actor. I put on a wig and a woman's clothes and make-up, and I stole the pram. Other children had disappeared in the neighbourhood, and everybody connected my child with them. Yes, those poor kids were like a gift from God to me.

"And then I killed my son." It was obviously the first time he had told anybody; Rolfe might have been confiding in an old and trusted friend.

"Can you blame me, Mr. Vanin? You came here to force me to betray my country, but, as a man, can you blame me? Look for yourself and then tell me. The last book on the third shelf from the top. That's right. Now turn to Chapter 6, page 89. Oh, yes, I know the place well, and I often look at that illustration." He watched Vanin's face and smiled—a very bitter smile.

"It's not pretty, is it, but that's what my son would have become if he'd lived. He was the victim of a pituitary complaint, and of a mercifully rare condition known as *Morbus Crassi*. The Roman nobleman from whom it takes its name was put to death on the orders of Augustus Caesar. He was only sixteen years old at the time, but before he died he killed two of the six men who came to strangle him."

"No, I don't blame you," Vanin replied. "I'm just very

sorry." He closed the book, for there was no point in looking further. The thing it showed was far, far worse than anything he had imagined possible and there was no point in looking at it. No point in studying those terrible limbs and the face that needed a French word to describe it. *La gueule*—the muzzle of a beast.

"No, I can't blame you," he said. "But why not have had it put into an institution?"

"And let the world know that I'd fathered a monster." Rolfe shook his head convulsively. "I couldn't bear that, Mr. Vanin. I couldn't stand the shame of it. We'd both longed for a child, you know—prayed for it for years. And then one day Dr. Fenwick walked into my study and told me how our prayers had been answered." Rather horribly, a single tear ran down his firm, set face.

"I lost my temper and kicked Fenwick out of the house, but he'd left his notes on the table and after I looked at them I knew he'd told me the truth. If he was allowed to live, my son would become like that." His eyes flickered at the book in Vanin's hand. "I couldn't let him live, Mr. Vanin."

"And you didn't tell your wife?"

"No, I couldn't tell her. She was a very sick woman and the truth might have killed her. I've never told her, and the secret has been like a barrier between us ever since."

"And that's what you were frightened of when you got Flack's first letter, Sir Martin. Not of the police knowing, but only of your wife." Vanin kept his eyes on the gun that was pointing at him, but it hardly seemed important now.

"Yes, only of my wife. With the little that Flack could tell them the police would have never reopened the case, but I couldn't risk *her* suspecting. She'd wanted a child so badly, you know, and she'd never have understood. No, I think it would have driven her mad." The automatic started to come up and his face tensed.

"And now, Mr. Vanin, I'm very sorry, but I'm afraid I'm going to kill you. You are the only person who knows the truth, and there's no alternative. I'll get away with it, too. My servants are loyal, and when the authorities find that you are a Soviet agent—when I tell them I found you going through my papers—they'll believe me all right." Rolfe almost seemed to be talking to himself.

"Yes, you're going to try to kill me, Sir Martin." Vanin's hand began to slide towards the little dummy gun, but at the same instant he knew it was useless. He hadn't remembered to reload after those shots at Murphy in the club lavatory, and there was no help there. Unless he was very lucky Mr. Murphy would soon be revenged for his lost hand.

He braced himself for a leap at Rolfe, to throw the medical book at him, but he saw that was useless too. The man's finger was already tightening on the trigger, and Vanin would be dead before the book hit Rolfe. Vanin just stood there waiting for it, and he felt no fear, but only a terrible weariness. Weariness and suddenly—

Yes, suddenly hope. For without any warning Rolfe's face was altering again. All the determination left it and was replaced by a look of complete astonishment. The fingers slackened from the gun, and as they did so Rolfe began visibly to wither. Like a fly on hot metal his body seemed to shrink and grow smaller; then he tilted forward. The curtain behind him tilted too and for an instant he appeared to hang from it. Then with a noise of tearing cloth the hooks came away and he fell to the ground with the folds of the curtain covering him, nailed to his back by the handle of a rusty dagger.

For perhaps five seconds—they felt like years—Vanin stared at the ravaged face of the woman who had saved his life, watching her kneel over the draped figure on the floor and listening to her curses. Lady Rolfe had overheard their conversation and, as her husband had foretold, her mind had snapped. The story was finished: her son was revenged at last.

And then Vanin ran. He ran to the windows, wrenching them open, and it was nothing to do with the nightmare figure behind him that made him go. Outside he had heard the sound of cars, and he knew that the hunters were out. All that mattered was getting away.

Yes, Rolfe was dead, and the story was finished. Vanin had done all that was expected of him and he could look after himself now. He hurled himself towards Kate's car and he knew he would make it. He felt like a giant freed of a great burden and beyond human injury. Three times he should have died, and three times he had escaped death. Now he was going home and nothing could stop him.

He raced across the gravel of the drive, hearing voices all around him and seeing lights come up, but he hardly noticed them, for he was going home. He was within five yards of the car when his knees seemed to buckle of their own accord and he fell forward. It was almost with surprise that he remembered bullets travel faster than sound and that he had felt pain before he heard the shots.

The room was bright and clean and smelled of antiseptic, and Vanin was waiting for death. All the same, for the time at least, life was good and there was strangely no more pain. He stared at the blurred figure by the bed, waiting for it to come into focus, and he smiled slightly.

I made a good run for it, he thought. *Even with my broken ribs I nearly made it.* Then his eyes cleared and the smile went out.

For he knew the man all right. He'd seen his picture a score of times and read a score of reports on him. This was the man at the top, Malendin's opposite number, though on the surface he looked almost ineffectual. The popular caricature of an upper-class Englishman with his tweed suit, bow tie, and the cigar stuck out over his grey moustache. He was effective though. Every inch of that heavy, overclothed body would be effective.

"Good evening," Vanin said. "I led you quite a dance, didn't I?" He had no idea of the time of day or how long he had been unconscious, but it seemed the only appropriate greeting, for evening comes before night, and he felt night was very close to him now.

"Yes, you certainly did, my boy." Kirk removed the cigar and lit a cigarette which he placed between Vanin's lips. There was something very gentle, almost fatherly in the action.

"All the same, we got you in the end, I'm afraid." Kirk watched Vanin drag hungrily at the cigarette and then removed it. "And now let's have a chat, shall we? By the way, my name is Kirk, and I think you can guess the department I represent."

"Yes, I know you all right, and I am honoured—sir. May I wish you a happy Christmas, General." Vanin found the remark amusing, but he couldn't force his face into a smile. Somehow the muscles didn't seem to be connected with the brain any more.

"Thank you, Mr. Vanin, and the same to you." Kirk held out the cigarette to Vanin again, and then turned and grinned at the man by the door: a tall, dandified man with a lot of gold in his smile. Vanin recognized him at once as a compatriot.

"You see, Igor," said Kirk, "my fame is worldwide." His grin swept back to Vanin as though he were a rare and valuable possession which fate had thrown into his hand. "And how is Colonel Malendin? In good health, I trust."

"Yes, he was well enough when I last saw him." Vanin suddenly seemed to look right through Kirk's features and see the face of Malendin behind them. These are the people who really matter, he thought. The people who control the earth. The politicians have a little hour, but it is the permanent officials—men like Malendin and this Kirk—who shape policy. Suddenly he hated them all.

"Good! I'm delighted to hear it." Kirk might have been responding to news of the health of a friendly business rival.

"And it wasn't a bad idea of his, trying to get your hooks into one of our top financial experts; might have worked, too, for a time. Yes, quite a change in your methods. The British Lion brought down by bankruptcy, eh?—More ways of killing a cat.... Now, would you like to talk to me, Mr. Vanin? Apart from the very end, we know the whole story, I think. We found

Rolfe with a knife in his back, and the wife had shot herself. They were both dead."

"Yes, they're dead all right." Vanin closed his eyes, and he knew that Rolfe had died because he was too trusting and far too confident. He had thought that his wife was upstairs, respecting his privacy as always, but this time she had let him down. She must have felt the tension as he had waited for his visitor, and she had crept into the little room behind the curtain and listened. Like the hall, that room had been decorated by rusty, archaic weapons.

And as Lady Rolfe had listened to her husband's confession something in her mind had snapped, and a knife ready to hand had gone home through the folds of the curtain. Perhaps after that had come one fleeting moment of sanity, and the gun on the floor had seemed the only way out.

"No, I won't talk to you, General," he said. "You know we never talk." Nothing mattered any more, but it seemed important to keep Rolfe's secret.

"I know that you *rarely* talk, Mr. Vanin, but it doesn't matter now. You see, you never had a chance. Whatever happened, Arabin would have given you away, and even if you'd broken Rolfe and got him to do what you wanted, we'd have pulled him in. We had all the details in your letter to Tanek."

"The letter!" Vanin's tongue ran against the capsule in his mouth. At least they hadn't found that. Probably they knew he was dying anyway and hadn't bothered to look.

All the same, if he didn't die—if the hundred-to-one chance came off and he lived—then he might talk. One slow, accurately given injection of Pentothal would help him reveal a great many secrets. He couldn't take a chance of dying unaided.

"You got Kate Reilly, then?" He hated saying that.

"Oh yes, we got Miss Reilly all right. To be exact we got her three weeks ago and she was one of the few who did talk." Kirk motioned to the man by the door. "Let me introduce you to the young lady who took her place."

He smiled at the girl who came unwillingly into the room. "This is my colleague, Miss Kate Martin." Kirk's voice hardened slightly. "And now are you going to talk to me, Mr. Vanin?"

But Vanin couldn't talk to anybody—he was laughing. He was roaring with laughter, rocking backwards and forwards on the bed, his eyes staring up at the girl's face.

"So that's it," he said at last. "That's how you got me. May I congratulate you, my dear Kate. You did very well. You fooled a professional, and I like to give credit where it's due." Once again he shook with laughter, and then he turned to Kirk.

"All right, General," he said. "You've won this round, but don't be too pleased with yourself, for there'll be more—lots more. You can't destroy me, because I'm not a man but just a little part of a great big machine, and there's always someone to take my place." His tongue moved, and he felt the little capsule tilt into position. Then he looked at Kate again.

And, as he looked at her, her face altered. It seemed to grow older, and rounder, and there were wrinkles under the eyes. The face of a woman who was very dear to him. A woman who would go on living if he died well and didn't talk.

"Shura, my dear," he said, but he spoke in Russian and only Trubenoff could understand him.

"Shura, I love you." Vanin gritted his teeth and prepared for death.

But those weren't quite his last words. All at once the room seemed to fade, and he was back on the cliffs above Mizzen Head with nothing around him except the fog, and the grazing sheep, and the three men hanging from their stone crosses.

"Lord," he said, remembering his passwords, the words of the dying thief.

"Lord, remember me when thou comest into thy Kingdom." The thing in his mouth burst like a blister, and the taste of cyanide was fire to burn away pain. The world tilted and began to swing out towards. . . .

www.ingramcontent.com/pod-product-compliance
Lightning Source LLC
LaVergne TN
LVHW051006080826
845145LV00009B/2479

* 9 7 8 1 9 6 0 2 4 1 3 5 1 *